The Puppet Wrangler

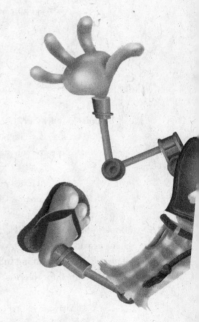

VICKI GRANT

ORCA BOOK PUBLISHERS

National Library of Canada Cataloguing in Publication Data

Grant, Vicki
The puppet wrangler / Vicki Grant.

ISBN 1-55143-304-4

I. Title.

PS8613.R356P86 2004   jC813'.6   C2004-900714-9

Summary: When Telly is sent to spend a month with her aunt
on the set of a television puppet show, she is shocked to learn
that Bitsie, the cute star of the show, has a dark side.

First published in the United States, 2004
Library of Congress Control Number: 2004100990

Orca Book Publishers gratefully acknowledges the support for its publishing
programs provided by the following agencies: the Government of Canada
through the Book Publishing Industry Development Program (BPIDP),
the Canada Council for the Arts, and the British Columbia Arts Council.

Layout and typesetting: Lynn O'Rourke
Cover artwork © 2003 Kathy Boake

In Canada:
Orca Book Publishers
PO Box 5626, Stn. B,
Victoria, BC Canada
V8R 6S4

In the United States:
Orca Book Publishers
PO Box 468
Custer, WA USA
98240-0468

Printed and bound in Canada

08 07 06 • 6 5 4 3

First, of course, to Gus, who makes
all good things possible for me.

But also to Romney, who is not Kathleen,
Buddy, who is not Mel,
Jim, who may be Bitsie,
and the entire cast and crew
of *Scoop & Doozie.*

You are all too talented, good-humored
and civilized to appear in a book like this.

—V.G.

1

IT'S NOT WHAT
YOU'RE THINKING.

Everyone was screaming.

Most kids were screaming in a happy/scared kind of way—like we were all on some giant Krazy Karpet or something. The little kids were screaming because everyone else was. Adrienne Handspiker—figures—was screaming for help. (Like that would do any good. Who was going to help?)

I wasn't screaming. I never do. I was just sitting there.

It wasn't so bad. Whenever things get that crazy, my head goes really quiet inside. It's like I'm watching TV with the sound turned off. Ideally, I'd be able to change the channel too, but that would get noticed. (Go too blank in the face and teachers start calling home. I didn't need that. And you can bet my parents didn't need that either.) So I don't fool around with the picture. I just turn down the volume. That's when I get some of my best thinking done.

Like right then, for instance. When everyone else was screaming their faces off, I was thinking about the English language. It has got to be the worst way to say what you mean.

Example: I say, "My big sister Bess took the school bus." You think, "Yeah, so?" You picture your typical teenager with a knapsack and maybe a nose ring climbing on and elbowing her way to a good seat by the window.

You don't picture this: Bess actually taking the school bus. Hopping into the driver's seat when Fred Smeltzer nipped out to check the back tire, yanking the door closed with that big old metal arm, and gunning off down Highway 12 like some cartoon maniac.

That's what I mean when I say Bess took the bus. Once you understand that, of course, the screaming follows naturally.

Even I was surprised, though—when I finally zoned back in—to hear everybody singing. Bess had them all going, "I have not brought my specs with meeeeeee," just like this was some field trip to Ye Olde Heritage Saw Mill or something.

I have to hand it to her. Bess never does anything halfway. She doesn't just steal a car and make a break for Mexico like an ordinary sixteen-year-old would. She steals a bus and takes twenty-seven kids on the ride of their lives. She gets everybody singing and laughing and making up stupid verses to "The Quartermaster's Store".[1] She even takes the detour down Sow's Ear Road so we can go over the bump that makes your stomach flip. Fred only does that the last day of school. Bess was all ready to do it twice in one day!

---

[1] From now on just assume that everyone means everyone but me and Adrienne Handspiker, who didn't seem to be screaming anymore. By this time, she was curled up on a backseat, chewing on the strap to her knapsack.

In fact, she was actually backing up over the bump—which feels even weirder—when Cody Hebb barfed.

Things kind of went downhill from there. It was hot in the bus anyway, and what with all the excitement and Cody throwing up whole unchewed pieces of bacon, everyone started barfing. Well, not everyone, but there was a definite trend in that direction.

Bess even managed to make that fun. She started a contest—sort of a Motion Sickness Olympics—and everyone (who wasn't busy throwing up) really got into it. She called it Digestive Tract and Field. (I was the only one who got the joke. Our dad's the town doctor.) She had one eye on the road and the other eye looking for technical proficiency and artistic merit. She gave Cody a whole bunch of extra points for those reusable bacon strips, but in the end Alyssa Corkery won. She'd had Tropical Punch for breakfast. That bright pink color was hard to beat.

Bess was just about to start the awards ceremony when we ran smack into the Mounties. Not literally "smack into them"—but close enough that even I screamed. (When the Mounties set up the roadblock at Hanson's Point, I guess they never figured we'd be taking the corner that fast.)

They sure looked pale by the time we came to a stop. Who could blame them? Bess was, as they say, "known to the police." They knew what she was capable of. They'd been bringing her home in the backseat of cruisers since she was five.

I guess it started out cute. I don't really remember her first run-in with the law—Bess is four years older than I am—but my parents used to talk about it. She was mouthing off—surprise, surprise—and got sent to her room. When they

3

went to check on her five minutes later, she was gone. My mother went hysterical. The Mounties found Bess an hour later, after Mrs. Sproule called (also hysterical) to report that someone had pulled out every single one of her tulips. Turns out Bess wanted to bring her mummy a bouquet.

See what I mean? Never halfway. Either lots of lip or 212 Princess Pink tulips, complete with bulbs.

Maybe if they'd nipped her behavior in the bud right then and there, the other stuff wouldn't have happened. (That's Dad's current theory.) But they were so happy to have her back safe and so "touched" by the bouquet, and everyone made such a fuss when Bess hit the front page of *The Clarion* (once when it happened and once when she helped Dad and the expensive landscaping crew redo Mrs. Sproule's garden), that the whole thing turned into an "Isn't-she-adorable!" story.

And there's always a bit of that in everything Bess does. (For instance, most hard-core criminals wouldn't have come up with the Barfelona Olympics idea.) When she mooned the politician, it was the guy who called Nova Scotians "lazy bums." When she ran away to Halifax, it actually was with the circus. Even her shoplifting was about playing Robin Hood. She just wanted to give stuff to people who needed it.

Or so she said.

There were times I liked Bess. A lot. She's funny and was usually there if I needed her.

No, scratch the last part. When I was a kid, she'd get me home if I was bleeding or wet or something. And believe me, if anyone ever dared be mean to her little sister, she'd stand up for me. (She always managed to pay them back double for anything they did.) But later? I don't know. Usually I just tried not to need her.

I tried not even to hear her. It was too confusing. I wanted to pound her for messing things up all the time, but then there's that other part of her. The part you just got to like.

I mean, like with this bus thing. Bess didn't panic even when we had to screech to a halt and two Mounties grabbed their guns and tromped over to the bus. They made her open the door and were all ready to climb on, but she wouldn't let them. "You know the rules!" she said, all singsong. "Old people get off before the new people come on!" That's what Fred always says. Everyone laughed.

Then, when the kids were all piling out, she reminded Ashlee Kirk to take her gym gear, handed Cody her own lunch (he was going to be hungry after losing his breakfast) and got everyone to give Alyssa the Champion a big cheer. Who wouldn't think she was sort of great? Even all the grown-ups who were bawling on the side of the road didn't look all that mad anymore. Their kids were all trying to wiggle out of their bear hugs so they could tell their parents what Bess did next.

When I got off, she fake-punched me in the arm and said, "Hey, Telly, don't hold supper for me. I'm going to be a little late tonight." It was the first thing she'd said to me all day. The Mountie snorted and said, "You're right about that, Bess. C'mon. Your mother's waiting for you in the squad car."

Waiting for her.

Mum arranged for Jenna's parents to take me home.

5

2

JUST SO YOU KNOW...

It doesn't run in the family.

I'm not like Bess. At all. I never wanted to cause trouble. I never even wanted to be noticed. I just wanted to fade into the background. I wore beige clothes, let my hair hang over my eyes and slouched.

That was the only thing I ever did that seriously bugged my mother. The slouching, I mean. I felt bad about it, of course—Mum had enough problems without having to worry about my posture—but I just couldn't get myself to stand up straight.

Maybe that was because I was twelve years old and five-foot seven and nobody that age likes to be five inches taller than the teacher.

But I don't think so.

I think it was because every time I stood up straight, this voice in my head would start screaming, "Get down! Get Down FOR GOD'S SAKE!" like I was going to get shot by some sniper or something.

I know that's a crazy over-reaction, but that's really what I used to think.

3

WHAT DID I DO?

You never know what people are going to do. Sometimes it's the so-called normal ones who surprise you most of all.

I figured my parents were going to go crazy. This bus thing was way worse than the tattoo Bess got on her neck or the words she sprayed all over her ex-boyfriend's father's Winnebago. Mum and Dad went ballistic then.

But here it was, two days later, and there was nothing. No yelling. No slamming doors. Not even any of that loud laughing Bess fakes to drive them nuts.

The quiet was making me nervous. Maybe this was going to be more like the time she got caught with a stolen credit card on her way to Sudbury. (She wanted to see the World's Biggest Nickel.) That time no one raised their voices at all. The family counselor got everyone talking, but even then Mum barely moved her lips. (It was creepy. I'd rather she'd just gone snaky and got it over with.)

I don't know why the whole thing was bugging me this time. It's not like it had anything to do with me. Just the same, I decided to crawl under my bed.

I make that sound as if it's something I only do in emergencies, like Dorothy and Toto heading for the storm cellar or something. But it's not like that. I really like it under there. I always have. You can still see where I painted the word "Dreemland" on the plywood ceiling. I must have been about seven. It was the brand name on my mattress, but it seemed like the perfect thing to call my little hiding place, at least until I realized that dreamland is spelled with an "a."

It's not as if it's anything special under there. It probably looks like most kids' beds, from the outside anyway. It's got a pink-striped ruffly thing that hangs down to the floor and behind that the usual junk you'd expect: a couple of old shoe boxes, a gym bag, a stuffed monkey. I put them there as decoys so my mother wouldn't get suspicious.

It's set up really nicely in back. Very neat. No dust. I've got a pillow and a little lamp. (It's an old bed so it's high enough.) There are books lined up against the back wall, a couple of games, my Discman and a picture of Snowball before she got run over. (Duh. Who'd have a picture of their cat after it got run over? Other than Bess, I mean.) Just below the headboard is my "kitchen": some juice boxes, some granola bars, two cans of ravioli and the can-opener my mother tore the house apart for. I don't actually eat anything under there, but I like to keep some nonperishables just in case. I also keep a change of clothes, though for the longest time they were size 6x because I forgot to update them as I grew. It didn't really matter. It's not as if I actually needed them. I just like the feeling of having my own little world that's got everything I could ever want, right there.

What's so bad about that?

I don't know. But Mum caught me crawling out of Dreemland once when I was nine, and I knew I'd never let her catch me again. Not that she was mad—what was there to be mad about?—but she didn't like it. She got that worried "how-unusual-dear" look on her face and then tried to make it sound as if I was playing under there or something. Like I was doing it for fun! I started pretending I didn't go there anymore.

No one knows I go there—though I figure the cleaning lady must have her suspicions.

Anyway, two days after the "bus incident," I was lying under the bed, wondering whether I should get one of those little pots to pee in,[2] when Mum knocked on the door.

"Telly?" Way too sweet.

"Just a minute!" I tried to sound calm but I was freaking. I thought she was going to walk in on me scrambling up to the surface.

"Are you changing, dear?…I won't come in." Luckily, respecting each other's privacy was one of the counselor's big things. Mum went on from outside the door: "When you're ready, could you come into the sunroom please? It's …important."

Important.

The Mercer family code word for seriously bad. But what had I done? Nothing. I figured it must be about Bess. Why did I have to get in on it then?

It hit me as I was walking down the hall. They were going to punish Bess and they needed a witness! They had to make an example of her. This was going to be like a public hanging

11

---

[2] Toilet facilities were the only thing I needed in Dreemland that I didn't have there. My big problem was I couldn't figure out how I was going to pee lying flat on my back. I must have known how to do it at one point because I wet my bed till I was nine.

or stoning or something. (Mum had been reading a lot of history books lately.)

No. It didn't take me long to delete that idea. My parents don't agree with "corporal punishment," so I doubted they'd go for an actual execution. (That would be overkill anyway. All they really needed to do was haul off and smack Bess— even once. It might have helped. At least Mum wouldn't be needing all that wrinkle cream now.)

(Don't tell anyone I said that. About the smack, I mean.)

(Or the wrinkle cream.)

I realized it was more likely to be an exile kind of thing. We were all going to stand at the door, pointing into the distance, and send Bess away. About time.

I was almost right.

Dad took my hand and patted it and talked in his nice doctor voice.

"Telly, we're going to send you away for a while."

4

SPARE ME.

Kathleen was way late picking me up at the airport, which kind of strained my relationship with the flight attendant.

Josette had really liked me on the plane. Why wouldn't she?

Braden, the other kid flying by himself, was such a pain. He kept on asking for more pop or a different Lego set or if he could trade in his half-eaten chicken meal for the lasagna.

Me? I was the perfect passenger. The quiet type who'd never ask for anything.[3] Josette could just smile as she went by and get on with handing out her headphones.

When she got stuck waiting at the airport with me, though, I knew Josette wished I was someone else. Maybe

---

[3] Parents go for that type too. I guess that's why I always got asked to lots of birthday parties even though I didn't have many friends. Bess, on the other hand, had lots of friends and not many invitations. The guy who drives the ambulance asked her to his daughter's party when she was little, but that was different. He knew first aid. (Good thing too. Before Bess had busted open the piñata, she'd beaned three kids and the family's weiner dog. And that was with a blindfold on. Just think what she would've done if she could have actually aimed.)

not Braden, but at least someone who talked. Even one of those kids who never stopped talking. In fact, given a choice between Bess mouthing off in handcuffs and me, I bet she'd have taken Bess any day.

I can't blame her. It would have made killing the time a whole lot easier.

In the twenty minutes we'd been sitting there on my luggage, Josette had found out I was in Grade Seven and from teeny, tiny Beach Meadows, Nova Scotia, and had a dead cat. She was running out of questions to ask. (The dead cat was kind of a conversation stopper anyway.)

She was going on again about how excited I must be to visit Toronto when I saw Kathleen come flying in the door. You couldn't miss that new red hair of hers.

I grabbed my fleece and started stuffing my book into my knapsack. I was psyching myself up to give Kathleen a kiss—Mum said I absolutely had to—when I realized I had a little more time to prepare.

Kathleen was about ten meters away, heading right for me, when she suddenly stopped and swung around. She stood there with her back to me, waving an arm in the air like she was Bugs Bunny conducting an orchestra or something. She stomped her foot a couple of times too, then leaned against the glass wall, that arm still flailing away.

I couldn't believe it.

Kathleen was on her cell phone!

Luckily, Josette didn't notice. She just kept going on about all the wonderful things to do, restaurants to visit, places to shop—like I was some little hick kid[4] who'd never been to the big city before.[5] I turned down the sound and disappeared into my head.

I started thinking about how different Kathleen and Mum are.

For starters, Mum would have been on time. No matter what. A raptor could have mauled her and left her for dead in the driveway and she'd still manage to drag her legless body to the airport five minutes early. In fact, by the time my bags arrived, she'd have written a note to the cleaning staff in her own blood apologizing for the mess she'd made. She'd also have come up with a home lesson plan on meat-eating dinosaurs. ("You can see by the wound how he was able to tear off my left leg with a single snap of his massive jaws. I wish you'd been there, Telly! It really was fascinating.")

She sure wouldn't keep anyone waiting to take a cell-phone call.

Even if she approved of cell phones. (Which of course she doesn't. Mum's generally against anything hightech. And that includes two-ply toilet paper and toasters that pop on their own.)

Mum and Kathleen look totally different too. Mum goes for that natural stuff. Her blond highlights look like the sun made them, and you can't even tell when she's wearing makeup. (Though it's kind of obvious when she's not.) Her clothes all come from catalogs in the States that show people chopping wood in their best pants or laughing when someone throws snow in their face. (Like any grown-up would do that.)

15

---

4 Okay, I guess she was right about that.
5 But I had been to Toronto before. Lots of times. Or once before anyway. Mum took me up as proof she wasn't a hopeless parent when she went to that conference for the Canadian Chapter of Responsible Parents of Irresponsible Children.

Kathleen, on the other hand, is kind of, I don't know, pointy or something. She reminds me of one of those Brain-Buster problems they give you on the so-called Math "Fun" Day. "Can you make a person using just five rectangles, a square and two rhombuses?" There are no circles on Kathleen. There aren't even any semicircles.

I know she looks good because people in magazines look like her. But I always thought she looked kind of scary too. Like the captain of the enemy spaceship in one of those sci-fi movies or something. They always have the perfect face and the really cool uniform. That's how you know they're evil.

Believe me, I'm not saying Kathleen's evil. (Mum would kill me if she ever heard me call her baby sister evil.) But she's certainly got the look down pat.

One last thing. Mum is Ms. Community Volunteer of the Year. If you're a homeless person or an ex-convict or some little sea slug that everyone else in the universe would be delighted to hear is about to go extinct, my mother is there for you.

That's really important to remember.

I know I made her sound kind of bad when I was talking about Bess, but Mum really tries hard. She really wants to believe that everybody (except the people who make artificial coloring and the guy building the condos practically right on the public beach) is basically good and trying to do what's best. She wants to make the world a better place.

Kathleen, on the other hand, is a television producer.

She makes TV shows.

We don't even have a TV.

That's because my mother believes that television is "mulching the minds of our children." I always figured she'd

16

disown me if she knew how much TV I used to watch at Bethany MacMaster's before Bethany realized that was the only reason I came over. (I know she'd divorce Dad if she found out he rented us a television whenever she went on a yoga weekend.)

Now she was sending me to stay with her pointy sister Kathleen to "help her out in the studio." She was even making it sound like it was a good thing.

Right.

And having your leg chewed off by a giant lizard is a learning experience.

Dad at least was honest. He did that whole "It'll be fun!" thing, but he also admitted that they didn't have the time to be worried about me right now. (Okay, he didn't say exactly that—but that's what he meant.) They had to straighten Bess out.

I was getting to skip a month of school, go to the big city and work on a TV show.

I was trying not to cry when I saw Kathleen accidentally thwack an old man in the back of the head with that flailing arm of hers and send him sliding across the floor like a big plaid mackerel.

Suddenly, everything started going crazy. Josette rushed to help, but before she could the old man took down a lady eating an ice-cream cone and a pilot who knew a lot of bad words in both French and English. A security guy came running over like this was a national emergency or something. I guess he didn't see the ice cream on the floor. He did this log-rolling-competition thing for a while and then took a major face plant. That's when the next pileup started.

Kathleen, meanwhile, was trying to wrap up her phone call and help everyone to their feet and hand out her business cards to pay for any damage and act all innocent ("Why, Telly, when did your plane get in?") and thank Josette for looking after me.

People were still slipping around on the butterscotch ripple when Kathleen grabbed my arm and a suitcase and headed out the door.

You'd think we'd have had a laugh about it then. Maybe we would have, but Kathleen had to take another call.

5

TELLY DEAR,

Here are a few things I'd like you to bear in mind while visiting Kathleen:

1. Never call her Kathi. She doesn't go by that anymore.
2. Never call her Kate. She doesn't go by that anymore either.
3. Call her Kathleen. (Not Aunt Kathleen.)
4. Be neat. Kathleen's not used to living with other people, especially someone who's almost a teenager, so it's important you don't make a mess. (Remember: Kathleen likes her magazines lined up with the corner of the coffee table. It's one of those funny things she can get a little "icy" about.)
5. Don't bite your nails. I know you never have, but it's a habit Kathleen can't stand so this would be the wrong time to start even if she makes you a little nervous, which she really doesn't mean to do. Some people just don't know how to take her.
6. Don't talk too much. I, of course, assured Kathleen this has NEVER EVER been a problem with you, but she reminded me how important it is to be quiet in the studio or when she's on the phone or when she's having one of her headaches.

7. Try and talk a little more. It's hard for someone like Kathleen, who's never dealt with young people, to keep a conversation going all by herself. So if she asks you, for instance, how you like school, don't say, "Fine." Answer with a sentence or two. How about: "Very well, thank you. I especially enjoy world history and music." This will give her something to build on if she still wants to continue the conversation and is not too busy or tired.

8. It's more important not to talk too much than it is to talk more. You'll figure it out.

9. Avoid telling Kathleen my feelings about the television industry. Even if she asks. Say nothing or, if pressed, lie. (I know that sounds unusual, but some day you'll understand.)

10. Be ready to go immediately whenever Kathleen is. (It's probably a good idea to leave your shoes on AT ALL TIMES.)

11. Don't worry about her driving. It seems worse than it is.

12. Try not to be in the bathroom when Kathleen needs to use it. She gets agitated if she has to "hold it."

13. Never argue with her. Most things will blow over if you just let her get them out of her system.

14. Try not to pick up any words or expressions your father and I would feel uncomfortable with.

15. And don't forget to have fun! This is a wonderful adventure you're going on!

Love and kisses to my darling girl,
Mummy

6

A FEW THINGS MUM COULD HAVE AT LEAST ASKED KATHLEEN TO BEAR IN MIND.

1. Try to remember that you have a houseguest. Do not forget to take her with you when you leave for the studio in the morning.

2. If you do tend to forget houseguests, make sure to have something in your fridge other than a small jar of Apricot-Kiwi Emulsion.

3. When it finally dawns on you at two in the afternoon that you're supposed to be looking after your niece and you race home and find that she's eaten half a jar of your expensive French skin cream, try a little harder not to look like your eyeballs are going to explode. Ask yourself these questions: At twelve, would you have thought that "emulsion" was a fancy word for yogurt? What else could she have eaten (since you went and left her stranded there)? What would her mother/your sister do if she ever found out? (Supplementary question: Why would you put face cream in the fridge?)

4. When you take a preteen to a television studio (or *wherever*), do not hold her hand. Especially when she's taller than you are. It makes her look like a goof.

5. Try to remember that you have a houseguest. Do not forget to take her with you when you leave the studio in the evening. You'd save everyone a whole lot of trouble.

7

i ALMOST DiED,

There were lots of things that kind of surprised me about the television studio when I finally got there.

For one, I wasn't expecting all the food. And I mean *good* food too. Muffins. Danishes. Chocolate chip cookies about as big as Frisbees, and I'm not kidding. Pop. Candy. Party mix. You name it. It was like a kid had done the grocery shopping or something.

The best part was that you could eat as much as you wanted whenever you wanted. It was all on a big table in the hall outside the studio and it was like, go for it. And, boy, did I. That apricot face cream of Kathleen's had made me feel kind of sick. (She got ripped off. I couldn't believe she spent $89 for it. There wasn't an apricot in it.)

Another surprising thing was how big the studio was. Kathleen produces this puppet show for little kids called *Bitsie 'n' Bytesie*.[6] It's about these two little alien guys who

---

[6] Ms. Pointy Producer doing a kids' show? I know. I was surprised too. I figured she'd do a news program or one of those lawyer shows where the judge doesn't like the hero, but he still always wins. What does Kathleen know about little kids? Other than they tend to smell and make poor fashion choices I mean.

live inside a computer and surf the net. Like literally "surf" the net, on surfboards. Ha-ha. How clever.

It's pretty lame actually. (You've probably heard the theme song. "We're caring and sharing in Cyberspace! So put a big smile on your Cyberface!" That's about as far as most people over three can get.)

There are, like, five puppets in the whole show. Bitsie. Bytesie. Rom. Ram. And their little human friend Amanda, who keeps on getting sucked inside the computer. (Like we haven't seen that before.)

Five puppets. How big a room do you need for that?

About the size of the school auditorium.

Honest. Maybe a little smaller—but you still could put the entire Beach Meadows Flea Market in the place. (Sure, the puppets are bigger than you'd expect—but they're not that much bigger.)

In fact, everything about the place was big. Big ceilings. Big doors. (You could drive a truck through them. Really. I saw them do it.) Big thick walls so no sound could get in or out. Big curtains that go right from the floor to the ceiling even though there's not a single window in the place. And big locks on everything.

Last surprising thing: the number of people who work there. Okay, like I say, five puppets. You figure five puppeteers, a camera guy and, if your aunt's a producer and you've ever heard of such a thing, a producer.[7]

---

[7] I don't know exactly what she does, but everyone sure does what she says.

Wrong. For starters, there aren't five puppeteers. There are only three. Christine, the lady, plays the little girl puppet. Jimmy and Norm do two puppets each. (They're kind of amazing, the way they can switch back and forth between different voices all the time.)

So there are fewer puppeteers than you'd think—but about forty more people than you'd expect. Three or four cameramen. Someone who decorates the set. Someone who makes the props. Guys climbing around on the ceiling making sure the lighting's right and guys crawling around on the floor making sure the sound's right. A bunch of people who look after the puppets, a bunch of people who look after the director and, of course, a bunch of people who look after Kathleen. And they're all running around with headphones on as if they work at the Gap or something.

And I'm not even counting all the people up in the control room who mess around with the computers and TV screens and stuff like that. Or the people who write the shows. Or the people who made the puppets. Or all the people I never figured out what they did. (It must have been something because they were always busy.)

The place was a zoo.

What didn't surprise me about the studio was that Kathleen would just drop me there and leave. She only introduced me to one person: Nick, her assistant, who is twenty-five or something, but is still so gorgeous that I was actually glad when Kathleen made him go with her. I'm used to not being able to open my mouth around people. It was kind of embarrassing not being able to *close* my mouth around Nick. He was so handsome with that brown skin and those white, white teeth that I just gawked at him like

25

I'd been hit really hard on the head or something. I might even have drooled a bit.

So anyway, Kathleen and Nick left and I was stuck in this big studio all by myself with a whole bunch of people. I was scared to move—and not just because I'm me, either. Someone else moved when the camera was going and this cranky guy named Mel went berserk.

And I mean it.

He started screaming, "Cut! Cut! Cut!" and telling off this props person for scratching her ear too loud or something. I never heard a grown-up talk to another grown-up like that in my life.

So there was no way I was going to move when the camera was rolling. My problem was that I couldn't figure out when it was rolling and when it wasn't. Sometimes, I guess the puppets were just rehearsing, but I never realized that until the camera started going again. So I just stood there and hoped that all the pop I woofed back wouldn't kick in and I'd have to pee.

I don't know how long I was standing there—except that it was long enough for Bitsie and Bytesie to do this scene a million times about being happy to have friends—when my stomach rumbled really loud.

I mean, really loud. Like a toilet flushing or something. Everyone must have heard it.

I was terrified. Especially when somebody grabbed me by the arm and whispered, "Come with me. Now!"

8

NO ONE'S WHO YOU THINK
THEY ARE.

That was Zola.

I immediately identified her as human. I just didn't know what kind of human. I mean, people in Beach Meadows don't look like her. Some people there dressed a bit like her—but they were all under five and their mothers made them change before they went out. That day, for instance, Zola had on long plaid shorts like your grandfather would wear, a little shiny mini-skirt (*over* the shorts), work boots, orange leggings and three tie-dyed tank tops. She had this rag—and I mean rag—wrapped around her head a few times. (That's why I didn't know that she was bald until the next day.)

And that was a pretty normal outfit for her.

It sounds weird—and it was—but once you stopped expecting something else, it was pretty cool too.

Kind of like Zola herself.

Hard to believe I was afraid of her at first. I had a good reason of course. I mean, she did grab my arm right after my stomach rumbled. (I figured Mel had heard the gurgle and he was going to kill me for ruining the "take.")

But that wasn't it at all. Zola had just noticed I was by

myself and was taking me over to be with her. We had to move fast before the cameras started rolling again.

I was still kind of scared of her even then because of the way she dressed. That's stupid, but it's true. It's like I was afraid she was going to start talking to me in some language I didn't understand.

Where did that idea come from? Like orange leggings and Grampie's shorts are the national dress of a strange foreign country or something? How stupid is that? (At least I sort of understand now why grocery clerks get all weird when they see Bess's neck tattoo.)

The truth is, Zola's probably the nicest person I ever met. Not in the fake way most adults are ("Aren't you a smart girl!"). But just nice, like that's normal for her or something.

Take then, for instance. She didn't have to bring me over to her workstation. She didn't even know I was Kathleen's niece, so it wasn't like she was sucking up to her boss or anything. She just felt sorry for me.

She didn't torture me with a bunch of stupid questions either. She just asked me my name (she even got it right the first time) and told me I could help her if I wanted to.

She's a puppet wrangler.

I know. Sounds kind of Wild, Wild West, don't it? Like she had to lasso and hog-tie them dang puppets or something.

Not quite. But she had to do everything else for them. She fixed them whenever they broke (which was, like, all the time). She made little costumes for them. She got them dressed and undressed. She cleaned and powdered them every night. (Even Jennifer Lopez doesn't have someone do that for her.)

(At least, I don't think she does.)

It looked like it was kind of a fun job. Most of it anyway. Zola had this big table set up that made her look like she was some kind of arts-and-crafts maniac or something. She had everything there: glue, feathers, paint, fake eyelashes, fishing line, chocolate cake mix—just in case they ever needed some "cybermud"—tennis balls, safety pins, makeup brushes, not to mention all these teeny-weeny tools for fixing the puppets' "mecs."

That's short for "mechanisms."

They're the little metal rods and things inside the puppets that make their eyeballs move or their ears wiggle or whatever.[8]

So, like I said, Zola had a pretty good job. The only bad part was that she was the person everyone got mad at if something happened to the puppets. Even if it wasn't her fault at all.

Which just goes to show you what a nice person Zola is. She went and rescued me that day even though everything was going wrong for her. The reason they had to do that scene a million times was that Bitsie kept breaking down. He was supposed to say, "You're my Bitsiest bestiest friend," but every time he got to that "bestiest" part, his

29

---

[8] They're also what make the puppets so expensive. Zola told me how much puppets cost and I couldn't believe it. Like thousands and thousands! I guess you can't just sew buttons on a sock anymore and hope the kids will all tune in to watch "Norman Foot's Big Adventure."

mouth jammed open and his little pink tongue slipped
out the side. He looked so human I couldn't believe it. It
was like he was gagging on it or something. Makes sense
now, of course, but then no one could figure out what
was going on.

It would have even been funny except that every time it
happened, Mel would go ape and Zola would have to race
up to the set and fix him.

Bitsie, I mean. Not Mel.

Though if you ask me, Mel could have used some help
too. Like a bucket of chill pills for instance.

Or a tranquilizer dart.

I don't know why Zola didn't hate the guy. He'd be pacing
around her on the set and looking at his watch and sighing
and yanking at his hair (what was left of it). As if that was
going to help. Meanwhile, Zola was doing anything she
could to get Bitsie working again.

And I mean anything. Even though she had those
special little tools, half the time she'd just have to Scotch-
tape Bitsie together for the time being so they could start
shooting again.

Mel at least always thanked her really nicely when she
was done.

Yeah. Right.

He'd just yell, "Quiet on the set! Let's go-ooo, folks!" and
make everyone get back to work.

But none of that seemed to bother Zola. First time I
saw it happen, she could tell by the look on my face I
thought the guy was a jerk. (That's another reason I liked
Zola. I hardly ever had to actually say what I was thinking.) She just smiled at me in that sleepy way she has and

said, "Don't worry about Mel. All floor directors[9] are like that. It's their job to get the show done on time. I'm just glad it's not my job."

She was even that calm with Kathleen. If you can believe it.

Take that first day, for instance. Mel had gone crazy at Zola for like three hours, and then the day was over and Kathleen came in and went double crazy because they were behind schedule. I thought Mel was supposed to take the blame for that, but because it was Bitsie who kept breaking down, Zola was in trouble too. Kathleen hauled them both off to the office like she was Mrs. Corkum and they'd been caught smoking on the school grounds or something.

Kathleen was tapping her foot on the floor and holding the door open (is she Mrs. Corkum's clone or what?), and even Mr. Tough Guy Mel was doing this "yes, master, right away, master" stuff.

But Zola? She just kept being Zola. She picked up Bitsie, asked the props lady to put the rest of the puppets away for the night and made me promise I'd help her the next day too. Then she said, "Okay. All ready!" and smiled at Kathleen, who almost smiled back.

Almost.

---

[9] Okay, this is confusing. There's a "director" and a "floor director." They're two different things. The director is the "creative" person with the "vision" for the show. You know—the guy in the cartoons who wears the beret and sits in the chair marked "Director" and starts to cry when Bugs Bunny keeps ruining Elmer Fudd's lines. He's too busy figuring out how the puppeteers should act and what angle the cameraman should shoot from and how big the fake spider should be to actually talk to the people doing the work, so he gets the floor director—that is, Mel—to give the orders for him.

But, hey, that was pretty good for Kathleen.

Once I realized that Kathleen wasn't going to kill Zola, I started feeling hungry again.

I went out into the hall to have another go at those chocolate chip cookies. By the time I'd filled my face and gone back into the studio, it was practically empty. There were just a couple of guys rolling up those big electrical cords that I was always afraid of tripping over. They didn't pay any attention to me, and pretty soon they left too.

I didn't know what to do. I had the feeling Kathleen wouldn't really want to see me right then.

I wandered around the studio. I didn't touch the cameras—I could just see me breaking one of those big boys and spending the rest of my life working at the Kwik-Way to pay it off—but I poked around the props table. It was sort of cool. Like someone had gone to a joke shop and bought two of everything.

Then I went and got a closer look at the set. The sets, actually. One was the straw beach house where Bitsie and Bytesie keep their cyber surfboards. Another was Amanda's room. And another was just a black starry background with big papier-mâché planets floating around. (That was supposed to be cyberspace.)

It was kind of cool, the way they looked so real. Amanda's room was just like a normal, bright pink, girl's bedroom—except it only had three walls (and of course the bed was fake). The beach house was like a real one too. (Like I've been to Hawaii and would know.) Cyberspace was just lame—but you get my point.

Of course the thing that I liked best was that the sets were all built about a meter and a half off the ground so the puppeteers could hide underneath while they worked the puppets.

32

I peeked under the beach house. It was just a concrete floor, but Jimmy, Christine and Norm had made it kind of comfortable. Like someone's basement rec room that their mother promised never to go into. There were pillows and magazines and old scripts scattered around. They'd taken a whole bunch of the blue Gatorade from the food table (I'd wondered where it went) and had hogged more than their share of muffins too. They'd also drawn pictures all over the plywood walls. (Some of them were kind of embarrassing. I couldn't believe adults did that kind of thing.) They even had two televisions down there.

It was like the luxury condo version of Dreemland.

I knew it was probably trespassing, but I couldn't help myself. I crawled under the set and lay on the floor. It wasn't as cozy as my place—my bed's only half a meter off the ground—but it felt good. Way better than Kathleen's spare room.

I lay there for a long time. I thought about Mum and Dad and Bess a bit, but not much. I didn't really miss them right then because I knew they didn't miss me. They had other things on their minds. Mostly I just lay there thinking what I would do with the place if it were mine. (For starters, I wouldn't leave those muffin wrappers all over the floor.)

I was just imagining what it would look like painted pale purple with red pillows when I heard noises.

A door squeaking open and then a voice.

"Let's gooooo, folks!!!!! C'mon! Are you deaf?"

It sounded like Mel. I almost barfed—but I didn't move. Or breathe.

He said it again—this time a little differently. "Leeeeeh-et's go, folks! C'mon!" I couldn't figure out who he was

33

talking to. The studio'd been empty for an hour and I hadn't heard anyone else come in.

When he said it a third time—"said," as in "hollered," that is—I thought I figured out what Mel was up to.

He was practicing.

Clearly, being a creep wasn't as easy as I thought it was. I figured it must take lots of hard work and hours of practice to get just the right amount of sarcasm in your voice.

Maybe that's what Kathleen told him to do during their little meeting, I thought. Work on his delivery. Develop his nasty side. Do what you need to do to get those lazy no-good puppets moving.

The longer and harder Mel "rehearsed," the more spit I imagined splattering around the studio.

No, that's not what I meant to say. (Even if it was true.)

This is what I meant to say.

The longer and harder Mel "rehearsed," the scareder I got that he'd find me there. I couldn't pretend I didn't see those "Authorized Personnel Only" signs. They were all over the place. I knew I wasn't supposed to be in the studio by myself. And I had serious doubts that Kathleen would rush to defend me, especially given the mood she was in.

This was bad. My parents couldn't take seeing both their daughters led off in handcuffs in less than a week. (Unless it was for an environmental protest or something, which of course this wasn't.) I figured I was doomed.

Until I heard Zola's voice.

"No, I'm not deaf, Mel—I'm just sick and tired of listening to a jerk like you anymore."

Whoa! I couldn't believe my ears. It was like Zola was a completely different person after hours.

34

I wondered why. Did something really terrible happen in that meeting? Or did she just finally snap? [10]

I didn't know what to think. (Other than "hooray!" of course. About time someone told Mel off.)

What confused me was that Zola said it again. And again. She tried it a few times, sometimes calling Mel a moron, sometimes calling him an "evil chimp-like being."

I actually started feeling sorry for the guy. Okay, he was a jerk, but she didn't have to rub it in. And it wasn't his fault that his arms were longer than his legs. (That might even have been why he was so cranky in the first place.)

As she went on and on about it, I started to think Zola wasn't who I thought she was at all.

Especially when, a minute later, a small blue alien crawled under the set with me and I heard Zola's voice come out of Bitsie's mouth.

35

---

[10] Being Bess's sister, I've seen my share of good people snapping.

9

Bitsie/Zola:

"EEEEEEEEEEEEK!"

Me:

"AAAAAAAAYYY!"

10

BY COMPARISON, EVEN BESS LOOKED NORMAL.

I don't know who was more freaked out. Me or Bitsie slash Zola. We just looked at each other and screamed for a while.

Then something happened that never happens in real life, but happens all the time on those lame TV sitcoms.

We both went, "What are you doing here?!?" at exactly the same time.

The puppet stood there glaring at me as if I just let my dog poop on his lawn or something.

My heart was pounding and my brain was really noisy. It was like someone in my mind was in a big panic, running from room to room going, "Do you know why this puppet's talking?…Do you know why this puppet's talking?" But nobody did.

None of this made any sense. How could a puppet walk and talk on its own? And why was it so mad at me? Maybe I wasn't supposed to be in the studio by myself—but I was pretty sure it wasn't supposed to be there either.

I decided the best thing to do was to act like this was all a dream, which I figured it probably was. I'd just play along with it and see what was up. That meant I had to answer him/her/it. (How hard could that be? Even I find it easy enough to talk when I'm only talking to myself.)

I said, "I'm here because it reminds me of my room at home. I have a little hiding place under my bed I call Dreemland. What are you doing here?"

Just like that. Nice and calm.

I was expecting Zola's voice or Mel's. Or even Bitsie's voice, I mean the kiddie one Jimmy uses for TV. Instead the puppet had this smart-alecky cabdriver-type voice. (Quite a contrast to his yellow fuzzball hair and the little sparkly hearts bouncing around on top of his antennae. It was like seeing a really short blue mobster all dressed up for Hallowe'en or something.)

"What's it to you?" he said.

I didn't let that bug me. I just said, "I told you why I was here, now it's your turn to tell me."

But did he?

No. He went, "Why would anyone lie under their bed? Can't your parents afford a mattress?"

I realize now that I should have said, "As a matter of fact they can't afford a mattress" and made him feel bad. But then I was thinking this was just a dream—so what difference did it make? I'd just talk.

I told him all about Dreemland—the food, the books, the clothes. I said how it made me feel safe under there, even though right until the moment the words came out of my mouth I didn't know that was how I felt. I didn't mean "safe" like someone was trying to get me—I meant "safe," the way you feel when your mother's actually relaxed enough to sit down for a while and you can lean against her on the couch and read your book.

I told him that sometimes I like to imagine living under there. I'd never said that to anyone before because, of course, I know how stupid it is. It's not like I'd really do it—lie flat on my back under a bed for the rest of my life—but sometimes I just liked the idea of it. It was so much less complicated than everything else.

Believe it or not, he seemed to be getting kind of interested in what I was saying. He sat on the floor with one little yellow beanpole leg crossed over the other. Every so often he nodded or said, "No kidding." He played with the heart on his left antenna as if it was helping him think or something.

Then he laughed and said we were complete opposites. I want to hide. He has to hide. He's dying to see the world. I don't want to see anymore of it than I absolutely have to.

41

That was true. He was making me think about things I'd never thought about before. I wondered if my *Dream Interpretation for Teens* book covered talking puppets. (The only things I could remember reading about were snakes in dreams and falling. I've avoided dreaming about them both ever since.)

We talked about a lot of stuff.

I said I was surprised he could speak.

He said he was surprised I could speak too. (A lot of people in the studio would be.)

I asked him if that was his real voice.

He asked me if that was mine. (Typical.) After taking a moment to enjoy his own witty remark, he admitted he could imitate the voice of everyone in the studio. It just took a little practice. (That's why he was working on Mel's and Zola's voices. Not that he needed to. He had them nailed.)

He asked me about my family. I told him the whole story. And—surprise, surprise—he loved Bess. He acted like she was a character in a TV show or something. He kept saying, "Then what did she do?" and laughing his head off about her popping wheelies on Mr. Zwicker's lawn tractor or putting so much vodka in Grammie's prune juice that she fell off the toilet. I didn't even feel bad about him liking Bess. I was just kind of enjoying making him laugh.

I was running out of Bess stories—if you can believe it—so I asked him about his family.

He looked at me like I was nuts.

"Family?" he said. Then he said it again, louder. "Fa-mi-ly?!?" His eyes were bugging out of his head like "You idiot!"

"I'm a puppet! How can I have family?! And who, exactly, would my family be?!?"

Normally, a mood swing like that would have thrown me, but this was just a dream, right? So I kept going.

"Well, what about Bytesie…or Rom…or Ram?" I asked.

You'd swear I'd just called his mother a hairless mole rat or something. He was so insulted.

"Oh nice!" he said. "I remind you of those…zombies, do I?!" He got this crazy look on his face. All he needed was some froth coming out of his mouth and an axe and he'd have made the perfect "Puppet from Hell." "Do I look…to you…like some foam-head who can't function until someone sticks a hand up my bum?"

I had no idea what he was talking about. But it was obviously something that meant a lot to him. (That's what the family counselor said when Bess kicked out the window in her office.)

"Do I look like I'm moving my mecs?!?" He put his hands up in the air like "I'm not doing anything!" and then crossed and uncrossed his eyes until I was worried he might get sick.

"Do you see Jimmy's hand anywhere down here?" He pointed his rear end in my direction and bent over.

Right over. So his head was coming up between his legs and he could get a good close look up his own empty bum.

He went, "Gee...I don't see anything!" like he was all surprised or something. He whipped himself back up straight, then turned around, really full of himself, like one of those TV lawyers who's just won his case.

"If you think those plastic dolls can do this on their own, you're crazy. They're just puppets!"

He was having a good little laugh at what a moron I was when I asked the obvious question.

"Then what are you?"

He stopped chuckling and tried to give me a "Can-you-believe-this-kid?" look, but I knew I had him. I didn't say anything. I just waited. After a while, he shrugged.

"Okay, I'm a puppet too. But I'm different. In case you haven't noticed..." Big pause. "I'm alive. It's not much of a life, I admit, playing Bitsie the Bonehead all day, then spending all night watching TV or finishing Jimmy's crossword puzzle—but hey! It's my life."

Gee, how sad was that. Even the old people at the Mayflower Rest Home get bingo on Saturday nights.

"Don't you have any friends? Someone to hang out with?" Suddenly, it was like I was his guidance counselor or something.

43

"You're my one and only, baby! No one knows about my special little talents but you. And I didn't even mean that to happen. As you know."

"Why not tell people?"

"Why? Miss Hide-Under-the-Bed-with-my-Best-Friends-the-Dust-Bunnies has to ask why? Because I don't want the hassle. Can you imagine what would happen if anyone ever found out about me? Everyone would want a piece of me."

Like he's so special or something.

"They'd all be trying to make money off me. Then I wouldn't even be able to live the crummy little life I have now. I'd be spending my entire life in front of the camera instead of just eight to four, Monday through Friday, with an hour off for lunch and two fifteen minute coffee breaks. If you think I'd want that, you're dreaming, kid."

That made me laugh.

"What's so funny?" he said.

"It's just funny to be dreaming about dreaming," I said, wondering if they covered that in my dream book. It probably meant I was dead or insane or something.

He gave me one of those "puh-leese" sighs.

"You're not dreaming."

"Yes, I am." I kind of laughed.

"No, you aren't."

"**Am too.**" He was starting to bug me.

"**Are not.**" He was serious.

"**Am too.**"

"**Are not.**"

"**Am too.**"

"**Are not.**"

"Am too!" I shouldn't have screamed, but I'd had it. I don't know why. It just wasn't funny anymore.

"Okay, I'll prove it," he said.

"Go ahead." I tried to say that the way Bess would have. Like "You and what army?"

Bitsie was enjoying this. He knew I couldn't back down. If it were just a dream, what was there to be afraid of? So he goes, "Take your index finger...Yup. That's the one. With the long nail..."

"Okay."

"And shove it up your nose...That-a-girl...Farther... farther...Get it right up there..."

"Ouch!"

I couldn't do it anymore. It hurt. And it was grossing me out too.

45

"See?" he went. "I told you you weren't dreaming. You wouldn't even have felt that in a dream. Proof positive: I'm as alive as you are!"

I wanted to argue with him, but there was nothing I could say. That guy in my brain started running around again, asking if anyone knew what was going on. Nobody had a clue. (In fact, they were all getting out of there as fast as they could. None of my brain cells wanted to stick around to find out what weird thing was going to happen next.)

I started to get really freaked out. I felt cold. And scared. I couldn't catch my breath. There had to be an explanation.

Think. Think. Think. Think. Think. Think. Think.

11
JUST SO YOU KNOW
PART ii.

I want to stop here a second and make sure this is clear.

I'm not prone to "flights of fancy" (Mum's term) or "hysteria" (Dad's). That's why I'm a "blessing" (Mum, Dad and most of the neighbors). They could always count on me to be "reasonable" and "no trouble." They know that one day I'll grow up to be a scientist or a librarian or some other boring thing that won't involve bailing me out of jail or apologizing to a whole bunch of people all the time. They don't say so—but I know they were kind of happy that my language arts assignments were always so blah. People with "vivid imaginations" write funny stories and commit crimes or come up with other ways to make their parents' lives miserable.

What I'm trying to say is that I'm not the type to believe that a hunk of foam rubber with eight fingers and a bright yellow Albert Einstein hairdo would talk to me. It just would never cross my mind.

So I knew there had to be a logical explanation for what seemed to be happening now. I told myself that, with the possible exception of Bess, there was a reason for everything. There had to be. I knew it.

I just had to focus. Stop panting and focus. I could see for myself that a puppeteer wasn't behind this. There were no electrical cords or wires coming out of Bitsie, so he wasn't a robot. We were definitely alone. And Candid Camera skits don't go on this long.

I ruled out any obvious trick I could think of. So maybe there was something about me that was making this happen.

But what? What did I do differently that day—other than, like, everything, that is?

Something must have happened. Did I hit my head? Did I inhale poisonous fumes? Was it something I ate?

Of course!

Why didn't I think of that before?

48

12

I'M TRYING
TO BE REASONABLE HERE.

"I'm hallucinating. You don't exist!" I was so excited. "There was something in the pop! Or ...or...or I overdosed on sugar! No, no, no! Of course!" I punched the air like one of those yahoo football players. "Kathleen's face cream! I ate Kathleen's face cream!"

It all made perfect sense—even if you didn't know Kathleen. Just think about it. The brain is all wrinkly. It dawned on me that those wrinkles probably had something to do with logic or sanity or something and if you did something to make them disappear—like eat anti-wrinkle cream, for instance—your mind went haywire. All of a sudden it just seemed so obvious.

You wouldn't believe how relieved I was. I just slumped against the wall and started laughing. Laughing, you know, the way you do when you think you lost your mother's watch and tear the whole house to shreds looking for it and then suddenly remember you put it back in her jewelry box before you went out and it was never lost at all.

All that panic for nothing. Even Bitsie's so-called proof of his existence didn't hold up once I thought about it logically.

"You're a hallucination—but the finger up my nose was real. That's why I could feel it!"

I figured that was the end of that.

Wrong.

Bitsie wasn't laughing. His eyes had gone blank, like buttons or something. His eyelids were half shut and he'd pulled his lips into this tight little "o." It was all very dramatic. I couldn't help thinking what amazing things they can do with puppets these days—or hallucinations for that matter. With that look I knew right away Bitsie was majorly p.o.ed.

People often act mad when they're really hurt. That much I remembered from our little family counseling sessions. And I could understand why Bitsie would be mad at me. I always hated it when Bess acted like I didn't exist. There aren't many things more insulting than that. Call me stupid, ugly or smelly and it hurts—but at least it's a pretty good sign that you noticed me. Even sniffing in disgust is better than having someone look right through you. (Maybe not—but you get my point. There's stuff you can spray on—or wash off—to smell better. What can you do to exist better?)

Anyway, I felt for Bitsie. I wasn't trying to be mean. I was just trying to figure out what the heck was going on. I was all ready to apologize to him—real or not—when he did the most irritating thing. Classic Bitsie.

Out of nowhere, he just threw one foot onto my shoulder, yanked himself up by my nostrils and sat on my head. My grunting and squealing didn't seem to bother him a bit. He just sat there bouncing his puffy blue feet off my shoulders.

I was ripped. Sure, I might have hurt him—unintentionally—but I didn't use his nostrils for monkey rings. I would have biffed him right off except I remembered how much

50

Zola said he cost to make. What with bus repairs and legal bills, my parents didn't need another expense right then.

So I took a long slow breath in through my poor bleeding nose. (Another little family counseling trick. Helps you stay calm.) I had no other choice. I told myself he was a person too, with feelings just like mine. (Okay, he wasn't a person, but I decided to leave figuring out what he was for another time.)

I let the breath out through my mouth.

"Fine," I said. "You have proved you exist. I just don't know how."

I guess that was good enough for him. He grabbed me by the ears and did a back flip off my head. I was supposed to be impressed, but there was no way! It's not like he had bones or muscles or anything that could actually get hurt. Any puppet who really wanted to could have done it just as well.

51

"Why are you hung up about 'how'?" he said, using the sharp end of Jimmy's pencil to unstick his left eyeball. "What can't they make these days? They've got cars that tell you which direction to go. T-shirts that know if you're getting enough vitamins."

"Yeah. But there's a reason someone would make those things! They actually help people!"

I shouldn't have said that. It just slipped out. It was like I was telling Bitsie he existed but didn't count. I thought he was going to give me that look again, but he surprised me.

He laughed.

"Yeah. I've got the same problem with that theory. There's not really much point to being me—at least as far as I can see."

"I know the feeling."

We both sort of smiled and looked away. We weren't mad at each other anymore, but neither of us was about to admit it.

"So got any other theories?" I said, figuring his mood had improved.

"Whaddya mean? About 'how the Incredible Bitsie came to be'? I don't know! How did you come to be?"

I wasn't sure if he was ready for this. But hey, I wasn't ready for a talking puppet. He'd just have to brace himself. "Well, basically, the female body produces eggs and the male body produces…"

I didn't have time to finish.

"Stop! Stop! Please! I've seen the Health Channel!" He made a "don't-make-me-gag" face. "You people look at puppets like we're the weirdos! At least we're not oozing fluids all over the place."

"Hey, you asked!"

"That's not what I meant. I was talking about the bigger picture. Not where did you come from. But where did the first egg and…whatever…come from."

I hate thinking about things like that. Mum and Dad fell in love, had Bess and then had me. That I can understand—though the part about having another kid after Bess always throws me a bit.

But trying to figure out how the whole thing started, how the first person started—that's too big. It's like swimming in the middle of the ocean. You could paddle around forever and ever and never reach the place you're trying to get to.

"Well?" he said, all smart-alecky again.

"I don't know. Some higher being made them I guess. God or something."

"And so why couldn't He…"

"Let's say She…" I can be obnoxious too.

"Okay, why couldn't She have made a talking puppet? It's not the strangest thing She came up with. She made platypuses. She made those hairless cats, not to mention people who actually find them cute. Hey…She made your Aunt Kathleen!"

We both laughed.

"Good point," I said. "So is that really what you think happened? Some god made you?"

Bitsie sighed. "Who cares?!? We can sit around here figuring out the meaning of life—or we can go out and actually try to live one."

On one hand, that sounded pretty good—in an Oprah Winfrey kind of way. (I could tell Bitsie was really proud of it too. Like he was Mr. Inspirational or something.) On the other hand, it sounded a lot like the type of thing Bess does.

By which I mean scary and/or illegal.

There was a long pause (by Bitsie standards, anyway). I figured he'd said everything he was going to say.

Oh, right. Like that would ever happen.

"Anyway, in answer to your question, I do have three theories about how I came to be. One: I'm a freak of nature. Sort of the five-legged frog of the puppet world. Don't look so shocked! I'm perfectly fine with that. If that's who I am, that's who I am. Theory two: I'm a figment of your imagination."

Oh boy, that made me mad. I practically attacked him.

"What?! You just spent all this time bullying me into believing you're real, and now you're telling me I just made you up!"

Bitsie rolled his eyes at me, which, frankly, no figment of my imagination would ever have the nerve to do. My imagination was the one thing I had any control over. Or at least I used to.

"Hey, it's just a theory. I thought you'd be pleased. If you ask me, as figments go, I'm way more interesting than your little under-the-bed world. Think of me as a sign you're improving!"

That was just mean and there was no way I was going to ask the little know-it-all creep what his third theory was.

As if I'd have to.

"Theory three: You're a figment of my imagination. That's the theory I like best because it means I don't have to waste anymore time talking about this crap." He gave me a phony smile and turned away.

Fine.

Jerk.

Neither of us said anything for a long time. Bitsie sat flicking his mecs. I cracked my knuckles. After a while it made me laugh. I couldn't help it. It was so obvious we were both just trying to bug each other.

Bitsie snorted too. I knew he was thinking exactly the same thing. He gave his eye mec a major yank and his eyeballs started bouncing around in his head like bingo markers. It was hilarious.

He may not be real. And he's definitely irritating.

But right then I knew he was my friend.

13
HE GROWS ON YOU.

We just goofed around for another hour or two. Bitsie even let me try puppeteering. It meant sticking my hand up his bum, but it was still a lot of fun.

Bitsie checked the time and made sure the night watchman wouldn't be around for a while. Then he hooked everything up for me. The camera. The sound. The lights. Everything. (For a puppet, he's pretty smart.) We crawled under the set and he put Jimmy's sweatband[11] around my forehead. It had this little tiny microphone attached to it. And I mean "tiny," like halfway between a Tic-Tac and a jelly bean. Sort of like a Cherry Nib but black and not as fat. I guess you could say it was more like a Licorice Nib but rounded at the end.

Anyway, you get the idea.

Bitsie taped a script on the wall in front of me, then turned on one of the televisions—though, of course, when I called it a television he made this big deal about it being a

---

[11] Ewwww...

"monitor." A Mon-I-Tor, as in "you idiot." He was shaking his head and snorting as if I'd called it a donut or a bicycle or something. It sure looked like a TV to me. How was I to know it only played back what the camera was recording? I thought the puppeteers were under there watching *Seinfeld* or something when they weren't busy.

I'm not even going to tell you what Bitsie said to that. He a had good laugh at my expense, then finally pulled himself together enough to explain that the puppeteers watch the monitor so they can see what their puppets are doing.

Bitsie attached these two metal rods to his hands and climbed up onto the set. I stayed underneath and put my right hand over my head, through the set and up his bum. He suddenly started screaming like he was in terrible pain. I yanked my arm out as fast as I could. I didn't know what I'd done.

Nothing of course.

Bitsie was just doing that to bug me. He couldn't feel a thing. I mean, he's a puppet after all! I was sort of embarrassed I even fell for it. How stupid was that?

When he finally stopped laughing enough that he could stand up, I tried again. I put my right hand up his body and into his head. My fingers were on the top part of his mouth and my thumb was on the bottom. That made him talk in a funny voice, sort of the way you do when the dentist has her hand in your mouth. He told me to take the cord that was hanging out of his insides with my left hand. There was this little springy thing at the end of it that looked exactly like the gizmo Dad has on his camera. The one he uses to snap family pictures when he wants to be in the photo too.

You know, that long cord thing. Sort of like a TV remote for picture-taking except it's attached to the camera.

Maybe you don't. Anyway, it doesn't matter. You don't have to know exactly what it looked like. It was just the thing that made Bitsie's eyes move. His eye mec.

Depending how you squeezed it, you could make his eyes blink or move side to side or up and down. My left hand is pretty klutzy for starters, so I was already thinking I'd never be able to do this. Then Bitsie made me hold the rods that move his arms with my left hand too.

According to Bitsie, "all I had to do" now was read the lines on the script stuck to the wall, move his mouth in time to the words and make him wave goodbye to his "friends at home." It was "easy." I just had to watch Bitsie on the monitor. I could see everything I was doing as I did it. I'd get used to it in no time.

Yeah, right.

Have you ever seen a video of baby giraffes? They try to stand up right after they're born, but their legs can't hold them so they keep doing the splits. Then they manage to get their bum up in the air, but their head's too heavy so their neck bounces around like they just lost a big prize-fight or something.

That's what Bitsie looked like.

No. Not quite. It was more like a cross between that and Frankenstein's monster. A very drunk monster.

With a limp.

And a broken jaw.

It was terrible. Scary, in fact. Can you imagine if Bitsie ever went on TV like that? All his little "friends at home" would be screaming for their mummies to call 9-1-1.

57

After a while I managed to get Bitsie's mouth flapping, but he didn't really look like he was talking. What he looked like was Grammie trying to chew without her false teeth in. I tried to get his eyes moving too. Most of the time nothing would happen at all; then suddenly one eye would twitch and you'd start to think that maybe Bitsie had a violent streak you didn't know about.

I felt like such a klutz at first. I couldn't even figure out how to read the script and watch the monitor at the same time, let alone move the puppet too.

But after a while I seemed to be getting the hang of it. Bitsie's mouth started to move in sync with the words, his eyes looked left and right and I actually got him to walk across the set without looking like he was recovering from a serious car accident.

I felt so proud of myself.

It was only when Bitsie started doing a perfect version of the Macarena that I realized I wasn't such a brilliant puppeteer after all. He'd been pulling my leg. He'd been doing everything for me!

It was pretty funny. Even I had to laugh.[12] I mean, who did I think I was? Some puppet prodigy or something?

We realized the security guy was going to be by on his rounds any minute, so we had to stop right in the middle of Bitsie's hip-hop routine. We rushed around and got everything turned off and ourselves back under the set just seconds

---

[12] Though not as hard as Bitsie did, of course. I was worried about his heart for a while there.

before the guard opened the door, poked his head in, closed the door and left. (Gee, some security.)

We just lay under the set for a while. I was tired, but Bitsie was still going strong. He could do the wickedest imitations of people. His one of Kathleen completely cracked me up. I know it's hard to believe, considering he was only a meter high and had big bulgy eyes and a nose like a beak, but Bitsie actually managed to look like Kathleen when he did it. It's probably because he had her walk down perfectly.

I thought I was going to wet my pants, I was laughing so hard.

In fact, I realized that if I didn't find a bathroom soon that's exactly what I'd do. Luckily, Bitsie had stolen one of the computer cards that unlocks the studio door. (He'd also stolen keys to the storage room so he could let himself in and out, keys to the control room so he could watch TV whenever he wanted and keys to Mel's car just to bug him.)

I'd just crawled out from under the set when I heard Nick's voice going, "Oh, good, exactly what I was looking for!" I thought it was Bitsie imitating him. (I had made the mistake of admitting that I thought Nick was cute.) I was just about to say something smart back like "Nick, darling, I thought you'd never get here!" when I heard footsteps. Good thing I kept my mouth shut.

It's times like that when you realize your mother is right about a lot of things. Like not wiping your mouth on your T-shirt after you've had chocolate chip cookies, for instance. It leaves these really gross stains.

They were probably the first thing Nick noticed about me.

59

14
EVERYTHING GORGEOUS NICK SINGH SAID TO ME THAT NIGHT.

1. "Tally?!?"

2. "You're still here?!…Ha-ha. I guess that's pretty obvious. I'm just a little surprised 'cause Kathleen left an hour ago to go out for dinner…How are you getting home?"

3. "You know, come to think of it, I bet she wanted me to take you. I've got a key. Yeah. I'm pretty sure of it. She's been so busy, you know, with the way *Bitsie 'n' Bytesie* is so far over budget and her trying to develop another series and all that. She must have just forgotten. Not forgotten *you*. Ha-ha. I mean, she must have just forgotten to remind *me* to take you home. I hope you weren't waiting long."(Adorable smile)

4. "Just let me get these scripts for tomorrow. Here—want to read one?"

5. "That's my car over there."

6 "Mind if I take this call?" ["Hello…Oh, hi!…Un-huh …Un-huh…Yup…I'm just taking Tally home… Kathleen's niece…Sure. Red or White?…Okay…Yeah. Me, too…"(Cute little laugh) "Bye."]

7. "So whaddya think? The TV business is pretty neat, eh?"

8. "I love it. Especially since I get to work for your aunt. She's pretty amazing, you know. I've learned a lot from her. I've got a series I'm hoping to get going myself one day, so this experience has been invaluable."

9. "Well, here we are!…You going to be okay until she gets back?"

10. "Look, ah, here's my cell-phone number. Just call if you need anything. And take this too. Kathleen never has anything in the fridge. C'mon. Take it. I've got a feeling you like chocolate." (Another cute little laugh) "See you tomorrow, Tally."

15

EVERYTHING I MEANT TO SAY TO GORGEOUS NICK SINGH THAT NIGHT.

1. "Actually, it's 'Telly.' My big sister couldn't say Teresa. In fact, nobody in Beach Meadows could say it—the way my mother wanted them to anyway. The Italian way: Tare-ray-sa. So Telly just kind of stuck."

2. "I thought I'd just take a limo—as usual."
3. "Oh, no. Not at all. It's given me a chance to study the sets."
4. "I'd love to. I'm a bit of a writer myself, you know."
5. "Whoa! Nice set of wheels!"
6. "Please do. I know what it's like to be waiting for an important call."
7. "Isn't that funny? 'Neat' is exactly the word I'd use for it too!"
8. "You have an idea for a series! Why, you're obviously extremely talented."
9. "Ha-ha-ha! Of course! You've probably noticed that I'm actually very...mature...for my age."
10. "You know, I like 'Tally' better than 'Telly' myself."

16

EVERYTHING I ACTUALLY SAID TO GORGEOUS NICK SINGH THAT NIGHT.

1. "Yes."
2. "Ahh…"
3. "Oh."
4. "Okay."
5. "Oh."
6. "No."
7. "Un-huh."
8. (I couldn't think of anything to say.)
9. "Un-huh."
10. "Okaythankyoubye."

17

MY DREAM COME TRUE.

I couldn't believe it. He gave me a Choc-o-rama.

My favorite bar.

And I'm not saying that just because Nick touched the wrapper. I always really liked them, even before I started thinking that he might have bought it on purpose just to give to me.

Or that he got it for himself because it was his favorite bar too.

Or that he really, really wanted to eat it until he realized that he wanted to give it to me even more.

I stood there in Kathleen's empty condo and just stared at it in "utter disbelief."[13] I pledged right then that Nick's Choc-o-rama would never leave my side.

---

[13] That's what Mum always says when the Mayor lets someone tear down a historic building, or the neighbors toss their recyclables out with the garbage or Bess puts firecrackers in the wood stove and "forgets" to tell Dad until he throws a match in and they start exploding all over the place. I always thought it was a bad thing until I realized that "utter disbelief" is also what you feel when it looks as if something good is actually going to happen to you for the first time in your life.

Suddenly, I was so thankful that Bess had stolen that bus. The family counselor was right. Sometimes the really bad things are what make the really good things possible.[14]

And what could be better than this?: "See you tomorrow, Tally!"[15]

That was the most amazing day of my life. A drive home with gorgeous Nick Singh, a script he selected specifically for me, and a commemorative chocolate bar of the event to keep for all time.

Right then, I couldn't think of anything else. Stupid, eh? I mean, which is more amazing to you? Spending fifteen minutes with some good-looking grown-up old enough to be your gym teacher? Or making a new best friend who just happens to be a puppet and the funniest person alive? (Okay, he's not a person and who knows if he's alive, but you get my point.)

I had to laugh at myself. It was all so great. Suddenly my life was full of happy stuff. Nick. Bitsie. Zola. Not to mention the all-you-can-eat junk food buffet. No doubt about it, things were definitely looking up.

I brushed my teeth, which is a really messy thing to do when you can't stop smiling, and I went to bed. I wasn't even scared to be by myself at night in an empty apartment in a big city. It was as if that chocolate bar would protect me. (And if you tell anyone I said that, I'll kill you.)

---

[14] Kind of like putting manure on your garden to make your flowers grow or something.

[15] It's even better than "See you tomorrow, Telly." It was like he had his own private name for me.

18
IGNORANCE IS BLISS.

I just don't get why anyone would want to see the future. That would be even worse than those movie previews that show you all the good parts before you even get to see the movie.

It'd ruin everything.

Take the day after Nick drove me home, for instance. Hey, take the whole next three weeks. If I knew what Bitsie was going to do or how many laws I was going to have to break and how many friends I was going to have to betray—etc. etc. etc.—I wouldn't have been happy.

Even if I knew for a fact that it was all going to turn out okay, I still wouldn't have been happy.

That would have been like knowing you've got a big test the day after March break. Instead of having fun while I could, I'd be worried the whole time that I was going to fail the stupid thing. Even though I never do.

Anyway, lucky for me, I had no idea what was coming. I had this crazy idea that bad things were what used to happen to me and good things were what were going to happen to me from then on.

For a while there, it even looked that way.

19
THE GOOD BITS.

Kathleen never forgot me in the morning anymore, mostly because by the time she figured out which black jacket she was going to wear, I'd already packed my Choc-o-rama and was waiting to go to the studio and see Nick again. After work, it didn't matter. I could get home on my own. Mum was always going on about how responsible I was. I guess that's why Kathleen gave me a key to the condo and a bunch of taxi vouchers and pretty much let me just come and go as I pleased.[16]

Of course that meant Nick didn't have to drive me home anymore, but I still got to see him about as much as my heart could stand. He used to come around to Zola's workstation just to talk to me and see how I was doing. I'd read all the scripts and I'd always figured out at least one good thing to say about them. (That was harder than it sounds.)

Of course that was a lot of thinking for nothing. I never did say much to Nick about the scripts.

Or anything for that matter.

---

[16] That – or she just couldn't be bothered about me.

But that was okay too. I talked to him a lot in my head. In real life, he'd say, "How you doin', Tally?" or "Havin' fun?" and I'd spend the rest of the day in my own little mental conversation with him. (When I wasn't working, that is. I couldn't just zone out the whole day.) I'd tell him jokes, talk to him about ideas I had for the show, sometimes I'd even have arguments with him—which would upset us both of course.

At least in my head.

I didn't say much to Zola either, but that didn't make any difference. She was "in touch with other people's feelings."[17] It was kind of nice being around someone who didn't need a constant "blah-blah-blah" going just to prove you were friends. And anyway, we were too busy to talk most of the time.

I'm not pretending I was a real puppet wrangler or anything, but I did do a lot of stuff. For starters, Zola and I went to the read-through every morning. That's when everyone sits around a big table and the puppeteers read the script out loud. It's kind of like a rehearsal.

Someone sat there with a stopwatch making sure the episode wasn't a second too long. (Okay, maybe not a second, but if it was a minute too long everyone went hysterical and started throwing out whole pages of the script.) The director listened to it all like he was Steven Spielberg or something. He was always saying things like "Can you try that with a smile in your voice this time?"

---

[17] Like mine about Nick, for instance, but she never even teased me about it once. Who else would pass up a golden opportunity like that?

Kathleen's job seemed to be cutting any lines that actually got a laugh. As I understand it, in little kids' TV, if a joke is funny, it's got to come out. Otherwise, someone might get "offended." I could tell this really made the writer mad. She hardly ever got a laugh, so chopping a good one must have killed her. She tried not to show it, but there wasn't much she could do about that big vein on the side of her head that would start throbbing like some alien life-form whenever a line got cut.[18] I guess she really needed the job.

Zola and I went to the read-through so we'd know which puppets and which costumes had to be ready for which scenes. (It wasn't like we didn't know already—but we went just to be on the safe side. You would too. Make one little mistake and Mel would go hairy.)

As soon as the read-through was over, we had to start shooting. We only had a day to do a whole fifteen-minute episode. At first I thought, A day?! To do a fifteen-minute show?! Like, What are you, lazy or something?

---

[18] I know this sounds mean, but I actually kind of looked forward to jokes getting killed. Not because the show didn't need a few laughs. Believe me, it did. But I just wanted to see that vein kick in again. It was amazing. Audrey – that was the writer's name – would be explaining why she thought the joke should stay and sounding like Miss I.B. Reasonable, but everyone knew she was seriously p-o.ed. I mean, the vein would get throbbing so hard that the big old hippie earring on her left ear would start dingling away like a windchime or a marimba band or something. I couldn't take my eyes off it, which is really rude I know. I just kept on thinking that if Audrey were my mother I would have encouraged her to wear a hat or a different haircut or even one of those big white bandages that cartoon people wrap around their head when they have a toothache. At least it wouldn't be as noticeable as that vein. What I'm trying to say is that it wasn't entirely my fault that I accidentally called her Artery instead of Audrey. It was really embarrassing, especially since everybody else started doing that coughing and nose-blowing thing you do when you're trying to pretend you're not laughing. I felt so terrible. It's hard to believe that Bess says that type of thing all the time. On purpose.

But that's just because I didn't know.

It takes for-ev-er to get anything done. You see some little goofball puppet pick up a banana on TV and it's like, big deal. You don't realize that:

a. It took the puppeteer seven takes just to pick the banana up with those little foam rubber hands and then

b. he kept dropping it so

c. they had to reshoot the first half of the scene (the part before he picked up the banana),

d. stop the camera,

e. get the puppet wrangler to tape the banana onto the puppet's hand and

f. shoot the rest of the scene as if it all went together, but then

g. someone up in the control room noticed that you could see a teensy bit of tape so

h. the floor director went nuts and

i. the puppet wrangler had to race back up and take off some of the tape—but not too much or the banana would fall off again—and then

j. they had to reshoot the scene, only now

k. someone else noticed a little itty-bitty flick of the puppeteer's arm coming out the puppet's behind so

l. they had to shoot the scene again, but this time, by mistake, instead of saying, "This is the best banana," the puppeteer said, "This is the breast banana", and

m. everybody started laughing (except the floor director who was screaming, "Cut! Cut! Cut!" and "Can we stop acting like bleeding children?") so

n. they had to shoot the scene again, except by now the banana had gone all brown and gross so

o. they had to untape it,

p. tape on a new banana (that looked exactly the same as the old one used to look because it had to match the first part of the scene) and then

q. start all over again.

(I'm not making any of this up. I mean, working on a TV show could be really fun, but it could be really boring too. I was just lucky to have Nick in my head, always anxious to steal a few precious moments alone with me. Ha-ha.)

What I'm saying is that after the read-through we had to boot it for the rest of the day. Everyone else got an hour off for lunch, but we usually just had to woof back some muffins (or in Zola's case this health food "snack" that looked a lot like something I used to feed my guinea pig[19]) and keep going. We were either trying to prepare for the next scene or get a head start on another episode.

I didn't mind. I liked it. I did a lot of the running around for Zola—you know, racing over to the organic grocery to buy herbal cigarettes so we could blow smoke out Bytesie's ears when he got mad. Or tracking down some old Styrofoam packing to stuff inside Ram the day his head kept caving in. (It's a long story.) Or finding a little sailor hat for Amanda when she got to be captain of the *Friend Ship*. (Get it?) That kind of thing.

---

[19] Wilbur died really young, even for a guinea pig, and I always wondered if I should mention that to Zola. I was worried she might actually be harming herself eating so many of those honey-sesame-nut chews. I figured she must have felt the same way about me and the chocolate chip cookies. She didn't say anything about it so I decided not to either. But I still worried.

I hardly ever did anything with the real puppets. Which is just as well. Can you imagine me trying to keep a straight face dressing Bitsie up as a stupid little cosmic cowpoke or something?

My job was to look after the puppet doubles. They're kind of like stuntmen. Nobody wants Brad Pitt to get hurt so they pay somebody nobody cares about to jump off the cliff instead. Same thing with the doubles. They look exactly like the real puppets—they're made out of the same mold—but they're cheap. They don't have any mecs inside so it's okay to throw them around or roll them up in a ball or drop them over the side of the *Friend Ship*.

I'd get the doubles in and out of their costumes. I'd take this teeny-weeny paintbrush and fix any little chips or nicks they'd get. Sometimes I'd even do bigger stuff.

Like once, when Rom's double got its head torn off,[20] I had to take it all the way across town to The Puppet Plantation. That's the company that made the puppets in the first place. It has all the molds and chemicals and tools you need for a big repair job like that. Laird MacAdam, the guy who owns it, looks kind of creepy—like going out in the daylight might make him melt or something—but he was really nice. He showed me all around the "shop" and let me watch while he put Rom's double back together. I would have loved to go back there, but every other time Laird insisted on coming to the studio to pick up the puppets himself. It was easy to see why.

---

[20] Bitsie's fault, of course.

He had a crush on Zola. It must have been a huge major throbbing crush because it was the only thing that ever got Laird out of the shop. The guy literally worked all the time.

So going to The Puppet Plantation was a pretty unusual thing for me to do. Mostly I'd just take care of the little stuff. Then, at the end of the day, I'd dust the puppet doubles with baby powder—that's so the latex foam didn't get all sticky—and lock them away in the storage room.

And that was when the really fun part of my day started.

20
MY DAILY ROUTINE.

I'd hide in the washroom or spend ages tying my shoes or look like I was really, really interested in some IMPORTANT PARKING NOTICE on the bulletin board. Then when everyone was gone for the day, I'd do the old "coast-is-clear" head spin and slip under the beach house set to wait for Bitsie.

It took him longer to get there than me. It's probably pretty obvious why. If worse came to worst and somebody caught me walking around the studio after hours, I could just say I was going through puberty.[21] If somebody caught Bitsie walking around the studio, they'd go nuts. I mean, you saw how I reacted when I saw him the first time. And I'm way more normal than most people.

So Bitsie had to be really careful.

Not that he always was, of course.

---

[21] I didn't remember that excuse until after my close call on the first night. It was an old Bess trick. Puberty made me do it! Like a little armpit hair would turn her into a criminal or something. It worked for a while, but now that she's sixteen she's got to come up with something new. Hopefully, before her sentencing hearing.

Sometimes he'd just make this wild dash for it like he was some brave army guy risking his life to save his friends. (As if.) Other times he'd climb up the walls and do this Tarzan thing on the overhead ropes and then just hope I'd catch him when he let go. The worst, though, was when he hitched a ride in the cleaning lady's cart. Just hopped on the bottom shelf when she wasn't looking and hid behind the Super-Flush cans until she stopped outside the studio. That was way too risky.

Which is exactly why he loved it. He could say he didn't want other people to know he existed, but frankly I was starting to doubt it. He was getting bolder all the time.

Anyway, when we both finally got to the beach house, we'd just hang around for a while. Sometimes he'd complain about the drippy scripts, but mostly we'd just talk about what happened that day and laugh our heads off.

Like I hadn't already laughed enough by then.

It surprised everyone in the studio when Kathleen's little deaf-mute niece started laughing all the time. But I couldn't help it. Once I'd found out about Bitsie, everything he did on the set was hilarious to me because I knew he was doing it on purpose. Like that first day? When he couldn't say "Bitsiest bestiest friend" and his jaw locked open and his tongue hung out like he was gagging? He was doing that on purpose. Just to amuse himself because the script was so boring.

It got even worse once he had an audience. He'd do anything for a laugh.

A lot of it was just plain childish. Whenever Jimmy put him down, Bitsie'd make sure his bum was right in Ram's face or his eyes were crossed or he had one leg bent up like he was a dog peeing on a fire hydrant or something.

Like I said, childish—but funny too.

What cracked me up the most was when he did imitations of real people right in front of them. I don't know how he got away with it. Someone would blow their lines and Mel would run up onto the set with his eyes all bugged out, yelling about how much money these sloppy mistakes were costing the production, and I'd look over and see Bitsie lying there perfectly still with his eyes all bugged out and his mouth stretched open like "You idiot!!" (It was hilarious, but I knew better than to laugh—at least out loud—when Mel was going ape.)

Other times it was way more subtle.[22] All Bitsie had to do was raise one eyebrow and he looked exactly like David Anthony Cudmore, the show's phony director. Whenever Nick would come around to talk, Bitsie'd do his bashful act. He'd look at the ground or make like his hand just happened to be pushing his hair back. I knew he was making fun of me, but I never let on. (I didn't want to encourage him, at least about that.)

At night, under the set, Bitsie would go through everything again, and somehow the jokes were even funnier the second time around. (How often does that happen?)

There were only two things that got in the way of our friendship.[23]

Number One: Bitsie watched too much TV. After about an hour or so of goofing around, he'd always want to go up

81

---

[22] That's the first time I ever got to use the word "subtle." It's one of Kathleen's words – believe it or not. She uses it to describe clothes and she doesn't pronounce the "b."

[23] Other than the fact that Bitsie was just a hunk of latex, of course.

to the control room and veg in front of the tube. The tubes, actually. He liked to have a different channel on each of the screens. You'd think I'd love that, not having a TV at home and all. I did for a while, but then it just got boring. It also got kind of creepy, the way he'd watch a cop show or sitcom or something and act like it was real. You'd think a puppet, at least, would know the difference.

That was the first thing. The second was worse: Bitsie was jealous of Kathleen.

21
IT CAME AS A SHOCK

Bitsie wouldn't admit it, but he hated the fact that I'd actually started to like Kathleen. It surprised me at first too. I always figured she was one more member of the family that I was just going to have to learn to live with.

Then one Saturday morning, when I'd been in Toronto about a week, she came up to me and said, "So what do you want to do today?" all sweet and everything. Or at least trying to be.

I'm not stupid. I know the only reason she was asking was that my mother called and wanted to know what the two of us had been up to, and Kathleen couldn't honestly come up with a single thing. (She's a pretty good liar at work, but she really can't pull it off with my mother. I guess it's the big sister thing or something.)

So that's why Kathleen was so eager for a little "quality time" together. She needed something to report. We looked at each other in terror for a while. I know she was worried I was going to say, "Why don't we go to the playground?" or "Let's make paper dolls!" or some other little kid thing like that. (Even still, Kathleen has a lot of trouble figuring out exactly what a twelve-year-old is.)

What I was thinking about, though, was Nick and how Beach Meadows I looked compared to him and how I'd like to find something more Toronto to wear. I just sort of blurted out, "Ah, could we go...shopping maybe?"

It was like I'd asked Bess if she wanted to help me steal a bus. Suddenly, Kathleen looked...I know this sounds ridiculous, but it's true. She looked delighted. Like thrilled. I barely had time to pack my Choc-o-rama before we were out of the house and on a major mall crawl.

I knew Kathleen was really worried about *Bitsie 'n' Bytesie* going way over budget, so I was surprised how much she liked shopping. It was as if spending money on clothes relaxed her or something. She smiled. She laughed.[24] She only answered her cell phone three times.

I was just planning to get one T-shirt (to replace the one with the chocolate stains), but Kathleen laughed at that too. One T-shirt?!? I called that shopping?!?

No. No. No. No. No. No. No.

I was getting a whole new wardrobe. And she wouldn't even let me pay for anything, even though I told her Mum had given me emergency money. (I wasn't worried about spending it. I figured if you're twelve years old and you have a crush on someone, a new T-shirt is an emergency.)

Kathleen insisted on paying for everything herself. I could be mean and say that was so I had to get what she liked—but it wasn't that.[25] She did it because of all the things my mum did for her when she was young.

---

[24] It was when I pointed out a jacket I really liked – but hey, she still laughed.
[25] Or at least **all** that.

She didn't say that exactly, but I figured it out pretty fast. She couldn't hide it once we walked into that store.

Kathleen was acting perfectly normal, I mean for Kathleen. She had her lip curled up, and she was picking through the clothes like they were somebody else's dirty laundry. She'd just said that there was "absolutely nothing here even worth looking at" when she suddenly sucked in her breath and put her hand over her mouth. I thought she must have forgotten something important, like her weekly massage or a dentist appointment or a niece left at the airport.

But it wasn't about that. It was about a pale pink sweater. The second she noticed it on the display she bolted over and picked it up.

No, that's wrong. She didn't pick it up. She "embraced" it, like the sweater had just come back to her from the war or something. I think she might even have had tears in her eyes. She started babbling about how the sweater was exactly the same as this one she really, really wanted when she was young. I knew the part about their father leaving them and Grammie not having any money or anything and how she took this horrible job as a secretary for this bad-smelling lawyer because it was the only way they could "scrape by." But I didn't realize that Mum had to look after Kathleen from then on.

Anyway, Kathleen wanted this sweater so badly, but she didn't have any money. She dreamt about it every night, but she knew she'd never get it. They were living on powdered skim milk and meat that had been "reduced for quick sale." There was no way her mother was going to spring for a pale pink sweater that would show the dirt and wasn't even very warm. Then one day, Mum—Kathleen kept calling her

"Dodo," which completely cracked me up. No one calls her Dodo. She's Dorothy—and you even have to pronounce the middle "o." Dor O Thee.

Sorry. Where was I?

Oh, yeah. Then one day, "Dodo" came home from her night job at the Burger Palace. Kathleen used to wait up for her because every now and again Mum would bring her back a "Queenburger" that someone had ordered by mistake when what they really wanted was a "Princess Pattie." [26]

That night, though, Kathleen almost didn't bother coming down because she couldn't smell any grease. (That's how she'd know if Mum had managed to scavenge some leftovers. Nice, eh?) But Kathleen didn't want her to think that the only reason she waited for her was because Mum brought her food.

So she ran down and gave Mum a big hug. [27] Mum had her hands behind her back and said, "I've got a treat for you."

You know the ending. No homeless Queenburger for Kathleen that night. Mum had bought her the sweater.

By this time, Kathleen really did have tears in her eyes. She said it was the nicest thing anyone had ever done for her. And it was especially nice coming from Dodo. (This was where Kathleen started talking in this really high-pitched

---

[26] You got to figure the food Grammie was feeding them was pretty bad if Kathleen would get all excited about a secondhand Queenburger in a soggy bun.

[27] Kathleen?!? Big hug?!? How badly did she want those burgers?

voice and swallowing a lot.) All sorts of guys[28] wanted to take Mum out back then,[29] but Mum always said no because she was too busy studying.

Kathleen said she did study a lot, but that wasn't the real reason Mum wouldn't go out with them. She was too proud to admit that she had nothing to wear. (The Burger Palace uniform just didn't cut it on a big date, I guess.)

But instead of buying herself something, Mum spent her hard-earned money on Kathleen. The money she had left, that is, after she'd paid for her tuition and helped Grammie out with the groceries.

Figures. That's just like Mum.

Kathleen managed to pull herself together. Boy, was that a relief. It was a nice story and everything, but I really didn't want to have to hold Kathleen up while she bawled her eyes out over a pink sweater.[30] I was already scared she was going to get mascara on it and we'd have to pay for it.

Kathleen just gulped a couple of times, though, touched up her makeup and we kept right on shopping. There were no more tears after that, but the stories just kept coming. Every little sock or hair band I picked up reminded her of something.

Like how Dad dropped into the Burger Palace for a Duchess Dog one day when he was at med school and

87

---

28 All sorts of guys??????
29 Take my mother out?????
30 She got me to try on the sweater, and I really liked it, but she said it wasn't my color. So much for being sentimental, eh?

then ate there every night for the next four months until Mum agreed to go out with him.[31]

Like what a good dancer Dad was.[32]

Like what beautiful curly hair Dad had.[33]

Like what nice long legs Dad had.

I was starting to think Kathleen had a crush on Dad, but I figured that was ridiculous. He was so much older than she was. It would have been like me and—hmmmm.

Oh. Right.

It would have been like me and Nick. I sort of laughed. Kathleen looked at me and sort of laughed too. Then she came right out and admitted that she'd had this big crush on "Mitch"—Dad, that is—for years.

Completely innocent, of course.

Of course.

Kathleen said I had to realize what it was like for her family back then. Mitch was like a knight in shining armor[34] rescuing them from this horrible situation. Their no-good father left them with nothing but bills, and then along came this kind, handsome, wonderful man. A doctor too—or just about! It was as if everything was going to be all right from the moment he bought that first Duchess Dog.

I could sort of imagine Dad making them feel that way. He must have been pretty amazing, I mean, before he lost his hair and everything.

---

[31] I guess after that many Duchess Dogs, anybody would go organic.

[32] This one I don't even like to think about.

[33] Dad had hair?

[34] She actually said that.

Kathleen could even be kind of funny. She told this one story about how, when she was twelve or so, she walked in on Mum and Dad "kissing." (There was no way they were just "kissing," but that's what she said.) Anyway, Mum got all prissy and flustered and said that Mitch—the doctor—was just showing her where her spleen was. (See what I mean? They weren't just "kissing.") I really laughed because I could just picture Mum doing that. It's like when I catch her eating Oreo cookies or ketchup chips or something highly unorganic like that, and she tries to make out as if she's doing some sort of scientific research on junk food or something.

That whole day we spent together was fun. Kathleen even took me to her hair appointment. They didn't have any openings, but Kathleen made a big fuss with the receptionist about all the money she spends there on dye jobs and facials and other things I don't even like to think about. The customers were beginning to stare, so the head guy promised to squeeze me in for a cut and blow-dry. I was sort of embarrassed about it, but when the poor little receptionist scurried off to see who could "do" me, Kathleen turned around and winked at me like "We did it, kid!" or "You and me, baby, all the way!" Something like that. I can't describe it exactly, but it was definitely a "we're buddies" type of thing to do.

We were both pretty tired when we got home, so we just flaked out in front of the TV. I was worried Kathleen was going to make me watch one of those old-fashioned shows about lords and ladies where they laugh at things that aren't funny and talk about things you don't understand. You know, your typical grown-up's idea of a good show. Something you could almost imagine my mother approving of.

Something even I wouldn't want to watch.

So was I ever relieved when she said, "Why don't we make a big bowl of popcorn and watch the Home Design Channel?"

The popcorn was pathetic—Kathleen doesn't take butter or salt—but everything else was perfect. It turned out we both loved decorating shows. And we both loved the really bad ones as much as the really good ones. (The bad ones are way funnier.)

We talked and talked and talked and I wasn't shy at all. I didn't always agree with her at first. Kathleen likes her rooms like she likes her popcorn.

Plain.

Or, as she'd say, "Simple, but elegant." (I'm the type that goes for the butter, the salt and the dill pickle flavoring. If I'd been rich and the type of person who liked other people to look at me, I'd have gone for a house with the works too.)

The more Kathleen talked, though, the more I started to understand what she meant. I actually began to see why those pouffy curtains were a big mistake. Or why that lady was smart to knock the wall out between her kitchen and her dining room. Or how a simple, deep grey velvet would have looked so much more sophisticated than that busy flowered fabric. I started to get really excited about how I could decorate under my bed, especially when that show came on about "Making the most of low ceilings."

I got so excited I almost told Kathleen about Dreemland. I said, "You know, I…" She turned and looked at me like she was really interested in what I was going to say. That's when I knew I had to change the subject. I didn't want to ruin everything by being weird. Telling her I liked lying under my bed. Making it like my own little house. What was she going to say to that? I don't know—but I knew what she'd be thinking: Get this kid out of here.

Kathleen kept looking at me with her eyebrows way up, so I had to think of something to say.

Brain panic.

Finally I said, "I...I think you should produce a decorating show. You'd be good at it."

I love it when things like that happen. When you just accidentally say the right thing. Kathleen's face got all happy. That's exactly what she'd always wanted to do! she said. *Bitsie 'n' Bytesie* just kind of fell into her lap, but she never really wanted to do kids' TV. She doesn't really understand children.[35]

Home design she understood. That's where her heart was,[36] she said. She was really working hard trying to come up with an idea for a series. The problem was "the market was flooded." There were so many home decorating shows already on the air. Kathleen needed to come up with one that was different, something with an "angle," a "hook" that the broadcaster would go for. You can have the world's greatest idea for a show, but if one of the channels won't pick it up, it's not worth much. Etc. Etc. Etc.

91

---

[35] No kidding. Though of course I didn't say that. In fact, I tried really hard to look like it wasn't even true.

[36] So <u>that's</u> where it was. I'm just joking. Kathleen has a good heart. It was just a little shy about speaking up. Can you blame it? Kathleen's head was pretty pushy.

She was really running off at the mouth by this time and I wasn't getting one hundred percent of what she was talking about. But it didn't matter. I was just glad to make her so happy.

It was like I'd given her a pale pink sweater or something.

Of course, all Bitsie thought was why didn't *he* get one too.

22

BITSIE AND THE
GREEN-EYED MONSTER.

Puppets can be so immature.

I went to the studio the next Monday and everyone had something nice to say. Nick said my new short hair brought out my green eyes.[37] Audrey, the writer, said red was my color, even though she had every right still to be mad at me for calling her Artery. Even Mel said, "What are you all dressed up for?" which doesn't sound like much, but from Mel it was a compliment. Believe me.

Did I say everyone had something nice to say?

I meant everyone but Bitsie.

I knew something was up from the moment we started taping the day's episode. Bitsie didn't try to make me laugh once. Even when Rom's eyeball fell out and Mel threw this big hairy fit on the set, Bitsie just lay there like he was brain dead or a puppet or something. That would never have happened normally.

---

[37] Even now, my heart still explodes when I think about it.

I tried to tell myself he was just tired or worn out. I didn't know. Maybe there was a puppet flu going around or something.

No such luck.

That night I waited so long under the beach house that I started to think Bitsie wasn't coming. I was actually beginning to get worried. I was just about to go look for him when he came sauntering in like he was the coolest guy at the video arcade or something. He went, "Oh, what are you doing here?" like I didn't go there almost every night after work.

I let it go. ("Letting things go" is another thing the family counselor liked to talk about. Sometimes it's just not worth getting into a fight.) I thought I'd tell him about my nice weekend with Kathleen.

Big mistake.

I told Bitsie about shopping for clothes. He said red brought out the color of the pimple on my chin. I told him about the hair salon. He said he liked the way my new do made my ears stick out. I told him about Mum and Dad. He said until that moment he'd been sure no one could be more pathetic than me and Nick, my little imaginary friend. I told him about watching the home decorating shows. He went on a major rant about how of course Kathleen loved that garbage! She was obsessive-compulsive! I pretended I knew what obsessive-compulsive meant because I didn't want to give him the satisfaction of getting to explain it to me.

As if that would stop him.

Mr. Health Channel went into great detail about this mental condition where people become absolutely obsessed about getting everything just perfect, and if it isn't just perfect they go completely insane. He claimed that Kathleen was the worst case of obsessive-compulsive disorder he'd ever seen.

That's when I decided to stop just "letting it go." What did he know? I said. Was he a psychiatrist? A psychologist? A human being?

No.

He was just a puppet who watched too much TV! He was just jealous because Kathleen and I actually had some fun together! That's why he had to put me and her and all my friends down like that!

There was no reason to be so mean! If Bitsie wanted to go to the mall so badly, I'd take him! All he had to do was say the word!

Me and my big mouth.

Instead of fighting back, Bitsie just went, "Okay."

"Okay, what?" I said, all ready to let him have it.[38]

"Okay, I want to go to the mall."

What could I do? I had to take him. I said I would.

95

---

[38] I was starting to understand why Bess always looked so excited about a big screaming match with my parents. For a while there, it actually felt kind of good.

23

AN EXCITING NEW
SHOPPING EXPERIENCE!

I was a little nervous about the whole thing. I knew there was no way I should be taking a $10,000 puppet shopping. But like I said—what could I do? I promised.

There was another thing too. I'd never had many friends before. Real friends, I mean, who weren't there just because my dad was a rich[39] doctor. Or because they wanted to have a good seat if Bess got arrested again.

Bitsie was annoying, childish and full of himself, but he was a real friend. The only reason he was there was me. He really liked me. I mean, why else would he get so jealous?

And I liked him too. He was smart[40] and funny.[41] I hated hurting his feelings, and this seemed like a pretty easy way to fix things. I had the taxi vouchers to get there. I had my emergency money. I had a knapsack to hide him in (as long as he promised not to step on my Choc-o-rama). And Bitsie had keys to get in and out of the studio.

---

[39] Yeah, right.
[40] Not as smart as he thought he was of course.
[41] He had no idea how funny he was.

One little trip to the mall. What could it hurt?

Nothing, it turned out. Bitsie kept his mouth shut as we went past the security guard at the studio, and I only had to shush him once in the taxi. (I told the cabdriver I had something stuck up my nose.) And even though Bitsie was really, really excited to be in the mall, he still managed to whisper.

Constantly.

But at least he whispered.

It was kind of cute actually. Like taking a three-year-old to the zoo or something. I thought he'd be really interested in getting out in the real world, seeing how people lived, how civilization worked, that type of thing.

But no. Bitsie was just interested in the stuff they advertise on TV.

98

He poked half his head and a few toes[42] out of my knapsack. He'd spot something down the mall and go, "Look, look, look, look, look, look!" all excited. "It's Donut Delite!" or "Casbah Carpets!" or "Mr. Big's Fashions for the Larger Man!"

Then he'd give me a major nudge in the ribs like I was his horse or something, and I'd have to trot over for a closer look. The whole way there he'd be singing the store's advertising jingle or repeating the special offers like they were this really important information. How to get out of a burning building, say, or what will be covered on Tuesday's Natural Science test.

Then he'd make me go into the store and try on the "Air-Pocket" running shoes to see if they really did support my

---

[42] There was no other place for them. Good thing he was so flexible.

arches better than other leading brands. Or buy a Fudge X-plosion Ice Cream Treat to watch the Pow-r Flav-r make my eyeballs spin. Or check out the patented Super Suktion of the convenient new Miracle-Vac. Sometimes he'd even make me buy stuff. Nothing he could actually use—like another tube of rubber cement, say, or some yellow fuzz to fill in that bald spot he had in the back.

No. Couldn't do that. That would almost make sense. Instead, Bitsie would beg and beg and whimper away until finally I'd break down and spend my emergency money on his very own glow-in-the-dark dog collar or bottle of Hyper-Wipe bathroom disinfectant or medicated bunion-removal strips for "greater comfort on your walk of life."

At first I thought Bitsie was just pretending to be so excited about these brand-name products. I mean, who really takes that stuff seriously? Then I realized Bitsie didn't have Media Awareness classes in school. He didn't have a mother who hated TV only slightly less than I hated turnips. And he didn't have anything better to do with his time. I guess if television was my only friend, my only teacher and as close as I got to having a parent, I'd want to believe it too.

See, that's the difference between Bitsie and me. I love TV the way I love junk food. I'm not supposed to have either, so I stuff myself full of both of them whenever my mother's not looking. But I don't think they're good for me. I mean, I might like having a caramel crunch donut with every meal, but I don't think they should be on the Canada Food Guide or anything. They're just junk food.

The same thing with TV. Even educational TV is just junk with fiber. Like those whole-grain tofu brownies Mum makes as a so-called treat.

When I want a treat, I want a treat. Something I can actually enjoy. Something that's actually fun. Something that has absolutely nothing to do with nutrition or education or doing the right thing. That's why I don't tune in to *Organ Overview* on the Health Channel to find out everything there is to know about my intestines. When I get to watch TV, I watch *Adventures of Diamond Eyes, Fang: Dog of the Undead* or—even better—*Summer Homes of the Rich and Lazy.*

I mean, it's just TV. It's a toy. It's not life. But Bitsie didn't understand that. I don't know why. He couldn't tell the difference between what was on TV and what was real. Seeing all those "nationally advertised brands" up close was a big deal for him. I wasn't going to ruin his fun by telling him the real story.

And it was only one little trip to the mall, right?

24

THIS IS HOW IT WORKS.

That was the plan. One little trip. But, well…

But, well, a lot of things.

For starters, Kathleen actually wanted to spend time with me now. I guess she needed a break from *Bitsie 'n' Bytesie*—especially the money problems—so we started to go out to dinner quite a bit. Sometimes we'd talk about Mum as a kid or the season's hot paint colors or how old I'd have to be to get blond highlights, but mostly we just talked about ideas for a new series.

Kathleen was desperate to come up with a home decorating show. At first I thought that was just because she wasn't happy doing kids' TV. Which of course she wasn't. But then she explained how the television business works. She figured if she was lucky, *Bitsie 'n' Bytesie* would be renewed for one more year and they'd make twenty-six new episodes. That would mean she'd have enough shows "in the can" to sell the series to other countries and, hopefully, make enough money to pay for all the budget overruns.

I figured, so what's the hurry? She had a whole year to come up with a new show idea.

Wrong.

That's not how it goes. Kathleen said it takes at least a year to get a new series up and running.

More likely two.

Often three.

Or even five.

That's because first you have to come up with an idea, and then you have to find a television channel that likes it. You have to get sample scripts written so they can see if it's really what they want. And you have to find a whole bunch of people to lend you money to get the show made. Then in the end, after you've done all that work, the people at the TV channel can just say, "Ah…no thanks. We changed our mind." And you have to start all over again.

102   If Kathleen didn't come up with a good idea soon, she could have a couple of years when she wasn't earning anything.

Zero.

Zip.

Nothing.

Having gone shopping with her, I knew how much she needed to make a lot of money. Kathleen was way past the stage where a secondhand Queenburger and a pink sweater would satisfy her.

That's why she was even willing to pay someone else for a series idea. She was actually ready to "buy" an idea and then produce it herself. Writers were coming to her all the time with proposals for shows, but nothing was really right. She almost bought a series idea about basement apartments called "The Lowest of the Low." She looked at one called "Colors of Contentment" that sounded a lot like mind control to me. The guy said he could make people happier just by painting their rooms the right color and drugging them.[43]

And I had to literally beg her not to pay this lady $5000[44] for a show called—wait for it—"Doorknobs." Kathleen actually thought a thirteen-part series on the history of doorknobs would be interesting.

Like I said, she was getting desperate.

Of course, every time I went out for dinner with Kathleen, Bitsie would get all jealous again. He'd pout. He wouldn't talk to me.

Or worse, he wouldn't stop talking to me. About what a babe I thought I was in my new "aren't-I-fabulous" capris. About how I must be too good for him now that I dined with Ka-th-leen all the time. About what a phony I was.

I tried not to let it bother me. I knew he was only saying that stuff because his feelings were hurt. I knew we were still friends.

So I took him to the mall a couple of times to make up for going out with Kathleen. Then, of course, I had to take him to the mall again when he caught me smiling because Nick said my shoes were cool. And again when Zola asked me if I'd like to spend a weekend at her cabin sometime.

Once I was carrying Ram's double up to the set and I tripped. Everyone had to wait a second while I rubbed my shin. Mel must have felt sorry for me because he didn't go ape about all the time I was wasting.

103

---

[43] I'm just joking about the drugging part. He was serious about the painting though. If that were true, I could have just painted Bess's room Cotton Candy pink, and life would sure have been a lot easier.
[44] Yes. Five thousand dollars.

To me, that almost proved Mel was human. To Bitsie, it proved Mel was my new boyfriend.

So I took him to the mall again.

I'd like to say those were the only times we went shopping, but they weren't. We started going practically every night that Kathleen had a meeting. The unhappier Bitsie was, the meaner it seemed not to just take him. I mean, I always made an effort to go out with Kathleen because I knew she was unhappy. Why wouldn't I do the same thing for Bitsie? He hated his work too.

Can you blame him? You must have a pretty good idea what Bitsie's like by now. Take a look at this script. Does it sound like Bitsie to you?

25

EPISODE 10:
BITSIE'S BIG SURPRISE.

BITSIE IS OUTSIDE THE BEACH HOUSE TALKING
TO A STARFISH A ROCK AND A BARNACLE LYING
ON THE SAND IN FRONT OF HIM.

BITSIE
Hello, Starfish! Hello, Rock! Hello, Barnacle!
So who wants to go swimming in the cybersea with me?

NOBODY ANSWERS HIM. BITSIE LOOKS
CONFUSED.

BITSIE (to himself, sadly)
How come nobody wants to play with me?
Hmmm. Maybe they're just shy.

BITSIE TURNS BACK TO THE STARFISH,
ROCK AND BARNACLE.

BITSIE (sweetly, so as not to scare them)
You don't have to be shy of me.
I'm not the itsiest-Bitsiest mean. I'm just plain Bitsie!
Ha-Ha! Now do you wantto go swimming with me?

JUST THEN BYTESIE ARRIVES IN HIS BATHING SUIT.
HE LOOKS AT BITSIE QUIZZICALLY AS HE TALKS TO
THE ROCK, THE STARFISH AND THE BARNACLE

BYTESIE
Hi, Bitsie!

BITSIE TURNS AND CLAPS HIS HANDS IN
DELIGHT WHEN HE SEES HIS BITSIEST
BESTIEST FRIEND ARRIVE.

BITSIE
Bytesie! I'm so happy to see you!
I want you to meet my new friends!

BITSIE POINTS TO EACH OF THE THREE
OBJECTS IN TURN.

106

BITSIE
This is Starfish. This is Rock. And this is Barnacle.

BYTESIE LOOKS SURPRISED.

BITSIE (CONT.)
They're going to play with us today!

BYTESIE DOESN'T WANT TO HURT HIS
FRIEND'S FEELINGS, BUT HE KNOWS STARFISH,
ROCKS AND BARNACLES CAN'T PLAY.

BYTESIE:
There's something very important I have to tell you,
Bitsie…

BITSIE TURNS HIS WORRIED FACE
TOWARD BYTESIE…

26

I WAS JUST TRYING TO HELP.

See what I mean? Can you get over how drippy that script is? And they were all like that. Even the nastiest *Bitsie 'n' Bytesie* episode made *Teletubbies* look like *I Saw What You Did Last Summer*.

So you can imagine how hard it was for Bitsie to act like he was that sugar-pie space alien all day long. It must have been an awful strain on him, pretending to be someone that nice.

It would be like Bess trying to impersonate Snow White or something. How long do you think she could pull that off for? How long do you think before the seven dwarfs would be paying the wicked stepmother to come get her?[45]

Bitsie was having a harder and harder time pulling the act off too. At least once a day, his eyeball would get "stuck" or his arm would get bent in some weird direction. No one could ever figure out how it happened. That's because they

---

[45] How long before Doc was prescribing the dwarfs tranquilizers? How long before Sleepy was having nightmares? How long before Happy had that smile wiped off his face? How long before even Dopey knew that Snow White wasn't as sweet as she was cracked up to be? This is almost too much fun.

always checked his mecs or his rods for the problem. They never checked his brain.

They never noticed that it happened every time Bitsie had to say, "You're my Bitsiest bestiest friend." And every time Ram said, "C'mon, Cyberpals! Group hug!" And every time Bitsie had to act like he didn't understand something your average newborn chimpanzee would have gotten right away. "No, Bitsie. When I said 'hop to it,' I didn't mean hop! Ha-ha-ha. I meant hurry!"

How humiliating was that?

So I'd take Bitsie to the mall. Make him feel better. Give him something to look forward to. I didn't feel bad about it. I figured even if the shopping trips were costing a lot of taxi vouchers and all my emergency money, they were worth it. They made Bitsie happier so

1. he didn't "break down" as much so

2. it wasn't as hard on Zola and

3. we didn't go into overtime as often.

It was a win-win solution. I told myself I was actually saving Kathleen money!

Unfortunately, I was also giving Bitsie ideas.

27
IT WAS BOUND TO COME TO THIS.

Like I said, he started off being good. He was quiet, polite and really, really grateful. After that first time we went to the mall, in fact, Bitsie actually said thank you! It was very touching. Like seeing someone who's lost a leg walk for the first time. (And it was probably about as hard for him to do.)

But little by little, Bitsie started getting bolder. He whispered a bit too loudly. He did stupid things just to embarrass me—like screaming "Hey, Handsome!" in my voice at guys who really weren't handsome, or making loud wet farting noises whenever I bent over to try on shoes.[46]

---

[46] He had a number of variations on this. Sometimes he'd follow the fart with a big sigh like "Ooooh, that felt good!" Sometimes he'd have me go, "Anyone else feel a draft? Har-har!" like I'm the type that would just let one rip in public and have a big laugh about it. Then other times he'd say, "Oh. Sorry, must be the sauerkraut I ate" or "I _knew_ those sardines I had for lunch were bad" or something else equally disgusting so that even though people around me couldn't smell anything, they started to believe that they did. And there was nothing I could do about it. If I looked embarrassed, people thought, And you should be! Passing wind in public like that! If I tried to look like I didn't do it, they all gave me that who-are-you-kidding look. That's the thing about farting. The more you try and deny it, the more everyone figures you did it. Nobody ever thinks to blame it on the puppet in your knapsack.

He also shoplifted. Or at least he thought he shoplifted. That's because I didn't tell him that the ketchup cups at Hamburger Heaven are free. I figured if he was happy taking them, he'd keep his four-fingered paws off the electronic equipment. I'd talk about whether it was right or wrong with him later.

All that was bad enough, of course, but then Bitsie ran away.

I didn't even notice at first. I'd taken my knapsack off and was sitting on a bench, resting. I was beat. There was a soap opera star at the mall and Bitsie had made me stand in line forever, waiting to get close enough to see the top of her head. (As if I cared about Schuyler Dawn Delano and her bouffy hair.)

Anyway, I'd been sitting there awhile when the old lady next to me got up and shuffled over to the escalator. I wouldn't have thought anything of it except she said, "Bye, dear. Nice talking to you." It seemed weird. I hadn't said a thing.

A moment later, it hit me.

That wasn't the old lady talking. It was Bitsie! He was playing another one of his stupid jokes!

By then, it was too late. I looked around and after a moment of pure terror saw the old lady at the top of the escalator. Bitsie was poking out of her Favorite Footsies shoe bag, waving and making faces at me, like "ha-ha, fooled ya." He didn't even seem to care if anyone saw him.

I have to admit that I always ended up laughing at Bitsie's fake farts and bad pick-up lines. It was embarrassing of course, but that's what made it so funny too.

This was different. This was way too risky.

I wanted to kill Bitsie, but I couldn't even get my hands on him. All the hard-core *Unbridled Passion* fans who'd stuck around to get Schuyler autograph were clogging the escalator. I tried fighting my way past them, but they were really tough. I guess you have to be to get those autographs. By the time I made it up the escalator, I was lucky just to catch a glimpse of the old lady's mauve coat disappearing into The Underwear Drawer.[47]

I ran into the store just as the salesclerk was showing her into the dressing room. I didn't know what to do. For a second I thought about sliding under the door of the old lady's cubicle, stealing the shoe bag and making a run for it. I'd have to hope she'd taken her clothes off and was too embarrassed to come after me.

It was risky, especially since if she was anything like my grandmother, she was past the point of caring. Grammie was perfectly normal and then she hit seventy and decided public skinny-dipping was absolutely a-okay. If someone took her new Favorite Footsies, she wouldn't think twice about engaging in a little nude wrestling to get them back. She would, in fact, consider it the responsible thing to do.

That scared me. I decided to wait until the old lady came out before I did anything.

It took forever. I wandered around the store, pretending I was going to buy something. The saleslady was immediately suspicious. I obviously didn't need a bra. I was too young (and not stupid enough) for most of the underpants there. (It was like Wedgie City. I mean, who wears that stuff?)

111

---

[47] "Intimate Apparel for all your needs – and desires."

The only other underwear there, I was too young for too. You know, the senior citizen gear. The bloomers. The girdles. The giant bras that look like two white bicycle helmets welded together. I figured that was what the old lady was trying on.

I hoped it was, anyway. It's stupid, I know, but the idea of her trying on a thong really bothered me. As if that was any of my business.

Finally, finally, finally, when I was sure the salesclerk was going to have me arrested just on suspicion of being weird, the old lady came out of the dressing room. By that time I had a plan all ready. I was going to walk up to the counter and stand behind her like I wanted to buy something. Then I was going to pretend to trip, land on the shoe bag and, in the confusion, stuff Bitsie under my shirt. I hadn't figured out how I'd explain the big squirming lump or the yellow legs dangling below, but it was the best plan I could come up with.

I was so nervous that as soon as I saw the old lady coming out of the dressing room, I grabbed the nearest thing to me and beetled up to the counter. It turned out to be a pointy, leopard skin bra with this feathery stuff around the cups. Normally, that would have embarrassed me, but right then it didn't matter. I had to move fast.

I was standing behind the old lady and was getting all ready for my big "accident" when she suddenly slapped her hand to her mouth and said, "Oh dear, oh dear! My shoes!" She'd forgotten the Favorite Footsies bag. She raced off back into the dressing room. (Okay, "raced" probably is a bit of an exaggeration, but she sure could shuffle when she had to.)

Now what was I going to do? The saleslady didn't give me time to think.

She said, "I'll ring that in for you while we're waiting."

Something else I hadn't planned on. Actually having to buy the thing! Bitsie needed that glow-in-the-dark dog collar more than I needed a 38D leopard skin bra. But I didn't want to make the saleslady anymore suspicious than she already was. I didn't want her to remember my face if anything I had to do in the next few minutes would result in criminal charges being laid against me.

So I just bought it.

"That will be $42.87."

I nearly died. I had no idea it was made of real leopard skin. It was going to cost me pretty much all the emergency money I had left.

I was fishing around in the bottom of my knapsack for the twelve cents I still needed when the old lady came back from the dressing room. I slapped the pennies on the counter and got ready to trip.

I was still struggling with whether I should throw my arms out like this was a major fall or just sort of casually stumble over the bag, when the old lady squawked.

I'm not saying that to be mean. She really did squawk.

Can you blame her? It must have been a terrible surprise, expecting to see a nice sensible pair of shoes in your bag and instead seeing Bitsie's blank eyes staring up at you.

"Good heavens!" she went. "What is this? Someone put a ...put a...goblin in my shoe bag!"

I could hardly trip on it now.

The saleslady started saying it was probably some sort of special offer. You know, one free "goblin" with every pair of orthopedic oxfords. That brought some color back to the old lady's face, and she started talking about what a clever shopper she was to have picked up such an "interesting" free gift.

She was warming up to Bitsie, I could tell. What if she took him back to the suburbs with her? Or mailed him off to her grandson in Pugwash Junction? Or got two dollars for him at the church rummage sale? Or let Bitsie talk her into selling her house and buying that state-of-the-art bar-becue system he wanted?

That last thought really scared me. Who knew what Bitsie was capable of? I had to do something! And right away too.

My mind was blank. No brilliant ideas. Not even any lame ones. I could only think of one thing.

I had to tell the truth.

I said, "Oh, no. It's not a free gift. It's mine. That's why I followed you up here. You were sitting next to me on the bench and then…"

Well, that's where the truth ended.[48] I babbled something about accidentally putting "my new toy" in her bag because I was too busy thinking about what I could get my sick mother for a going-away present since she had to spend the next seven to twelve weeks in a hospital that was very far away from our home, in a whole other country actually, and she might never see me again because there was always the chance the surgery would leave her blind.

---

[48] Just as well, all things considered. If I told the truth I'd be writing this from the loony bin.

I think the old lady gave me Bitsie back just so I'd shut up. Who knows? Anyway, it worked. She handed him to me and I ran.

I had about eight seconds of relief before I heard the saleslady scream.

"Stop! Stop!! Somebody stop that girl!"

28

IT COULD HAVE BEEN WORSE.

My heart was pounding. I couldn't let them catch me! I had to get Bitsie back to the studio—no matter what. I slung him under my arm like a football and picked up speed.

I ran to the left. Eight large Schuyler Dawn Delano fans formed a human wall and blocked my way.

I darted right. The saleslady was coming straight for me, all red in the face and screaming, "Hey, you! Stop! Stop!"

I swung around, hoping I could bolt down the escalator. No such luck. The old lady had read my mind. She'd wedged herself like a cork in the opening to the escalator. She was bent over with her hands on her knees, getting ready to charge. She was sweating and panting, but I knew she could still take me down easily.

I hesitated for a moment. But that was all she needed. The old lady pounced, slid across the floor and grabbed me by the ankle. "I got the girl!" she screamed. People in the crowd went crazy. It was as if Canada had just won the ten-thousand-meter relay or something. What could I do? I quit trying to drag her off with me and just gave up.

The saleslady did a few high fives with shoppers, then hobbled over to us on her broken slingbacks. "Good work, Mrs. Mancini," she said—then turned to me.

I figured I was done for. But the saleslady just smiled, handed me a bag and said, "You forgot your bra, dear."

29
HE DESERVED IT.

Bitsie was sitting on a toilet in the mall's public washroom. He was wearing my leopard skin bra and laughing his head off.

I was not laughing.

I was standing against the cubicle door with my arms folded, glaring at him. I had never been so angry in my life.

He was giving a detailed and extremely "humorous"[49] account of the chase scene. Like this was just some funny little prank that he'd rigged up for our amusement.

I let him have his fun for a while—and then I ripped into him. I told him he was thoughtless and selfish and just plain stupid. I asked him what he thought would have happened if I hadn't tracked that old lady down. What would have happened if she'd taken him back to her little retirement home and put him in her shoe closet, miles and miles and miles away from the studio? What would have happened if she'd opened her bag and looked at Bitsie and actually had a heart attack?

---

[49] At least that's what he thought.

"Oh, lighten up," he said. "It didn't happen, did it?"

Can you believe it?!

I went wiggy. I mean, even Mel would have been proud. I said, "What is the matter with you? Don't you realize you could have gotten lost, and the whole production would have had to shut down?"

He shrugged and said, "They'd just make a new puppet. It's not like they don't have the molds or anything."

"And who would pay for that?" I was practically screaming by this time.

"I dunno." Like, who cares?

I told him I'd have to pay for it. Once I got out of jail, that is. But even that didn't seem to faze him. Bitsie kept on looking at me like I couldn't take a joke or something.

That's when I knew I didn't have any other choice. I said, "I'm never taking you to the mall. Ever. Again."

Now that fazed him.

Suddenly, he was so, soooo sorry. He realized what a stupid thing he'd done. He was ashamed. Embarrassed. But reformed! A different puppet. He'd learned from his mistakes. He would never do anything like that again. Ever. He promised.

Like I was going to fall for that.

I said, "I know you'll never do it again. Because you'll never have the chance. I repeat, I am never, ever taking you to the mall again."

Bitsie was shocked. How mean could I be? He started begging for mercy. He told me this sad, sad story about how horrible it was to be in that little cubicle with a naked lady. He'd never seen anything like it before, even on the Health Channel. The whole time he was cowering in the corner, terrified. The shock was such that he could feel all his powers of speech and movement draining away from him. Numbing him. Reducing him to a simple foam-head.

The whole experience was awful, he said. Awful!

Oh, cry me a river. Like having to watch an old lady put on a girdle is the worst thing that's ever happened to anybody. Bitsie had absolutely no appreciation for what other people go through. He wasn't getting any sympathy from me. I just looked at him like "So what?"

But that didn't stop him. He had one more thing to try.

He stood up and stretched his hands out toward me. I knew he was going for that "sad but dignified" look, but he missed it by a mile. (It might have helped if he'd taken off that stupid leopard skin bra.)

121

"Haven't I suffered enough?" he said, in this pathetic little whisper. "The remorse…the fear…the never knowing if I'd see my loved ones again? What more can I do? What more can I give? If we are to live together—if civilization is to survive!—we must embrace forgiveness! And that's all I'm asking for. A little…forgiveness."

"Very moving," I said. "It's just too bad that we watched that episode of *Quest for Justice* together or I might have fallen for it."

Bitsie didn't have time to say anything else. I'd had enough. I grabbed him, stuffed him into my knapsack and took him back to the studio in silence.

I never even stopped to consider what all those ladies in the other toilet stalls must have been thinking.

30
REVENGE IS SWEET.

The next day was a Friday.

It was bad from the moment I got up. Getting ready to go, I realized I'd bent Nick's Choc-o-rama when I stuffed Bitsie into my knapsack the night before. I tried to be mature about it. It was only a chocolate bar after all, and it's not like I'd lost it or anything, but it was still really upsetting.

Then Kathleen got mad at me for keeping her waiting, even though I was the one who'd been waiting for her. (I mean, who absolutely had to find her Mulberry Gash Lip Stain that day despite having twenty-six other lipsticks to choose from? Me or her?) I kept my mouth shut though. I knew she'd been talking money with her accountant the night before so I was sort of prepared for her to be cranky. Not that cranky, of course, but cranky.

Even Zola wasn't herself. Her boyfriend's band—"The Tofu Weiners"[50]—had a big concert in Ottawa that weekend and the bus was leaving right at six. Zola was worried that if things didn't go smoothly on set that day, she'd miss

---

[50] The name suited them perfectly.

it. She was still nice of course, but I could tell she was anxious. And that made me anxious. When I saw Zola, a.k.a. Granola Girl, woof down that chocolate jelly donut, I really started to worry for her.

And it only got worse as the day went on—because of Bitsie. Of course.

He was acting like a complete jerk. He kept "breaking down." He must have done it ten times by noon. We were way, way behind and bound to go into overtime. That was bad for Zola—and for Kathleen. Kathleen had to pay everyone extra when things ran late. She wasn't going to be very happy about it.

I knew why Bitsie was breaking down of course. It was his way of getting back at me for not taking him to the mall.

It worked.

It was the perfect revenge. He could hurt me by hurting my friends. I didn't know what to do. Make us all suffer or just give in and promise to take Bitsie shopping again? It was the type of thing I would have liked to talk over with the family counselor.

I was agonizing about what to do when Nick came by. Bitsie's behavior suddenly didn't seem so important. After all, I was wearing the lime green T-shirt Nick always raved about ("Matches your eyes"). That day, though, he didn't even notice. He just rattled off a bunch of orders to Zola from Kathleen, and then, like it was just another message, said, "Oh, and Tally, there's an e-mail for you from your sister. It's marked urgent."

I told you the day stunk.

124

30
LETTER BOMB.

Zola said I better go to the office and check out the e-mail. I said no, I'd stay. There was too much work to do. I couldn't leave it all to her.

"No, no. Go," she said. "You have to. It could be an emergency. You shouldn't put aside your own needs for someone else's."

Did that ever make me feel like a jerk.

Zola was acting like I was so nice when nice had nothing to do with it. The only reason I wanted to stay was because I hated getting mail from my family. It always made me feel mad or sad or—worse—both.

Mum's letters always sounded great. "My dearest little Telly." "Darling Telly." "Sweetheart." She wrote just about every day by hand on paper, in an envelope with a stamp. Like this was the olden days or something. Who would take the time to do that nowadays? I had to admit that that alone was probably a pretty good sign she loved me.

She always gave me the complete weather report and the minutes from whatever volunteer meeting she just came back from and lots of news about how everyone was doing:

Dad is exhausted. Fern Haliburton went into heavy labor at two yesterday afternoon and didn't give birth until 11:30 this morning. She said some atrocious things about her husband and other well-known members of the community, but Dad said that was just the pain talking and it's hardly grounds for divorce.

Grammie has been playing a lot of bridge lately. She has a new friend who seems to be as devoted to the game as she. I do hope that she'll introduce us to this mystery man soon, at least before they go off on that little trip together.

Dad and I are feeling very optimistic about Bess. We've had some spirited interactions with her and have come to believe that her energy and passion will in the long run serve her well.

126

What's so bad about that?

Anyone else would say nothing. I was probably just being really childish and self-centered, but I couldn't help it. Every time I read one of Mum's letters I remembered that week I had to look after Mrs. Longaphy's cat. She absolutely loved that cat. Cuddles. She gave me these really long instructions about how to prepare his food, how often to clean his litter box, how to do his hair and how to pet him. He liked the fur between his ears all ruffled up and then smoothed back down with long, slow strokes. Mrs. Longaphy was worried that Cuddles would be really lonely,[51] so I had to promise to

---

[51] She almost didn't go to her own daughter's wedding, worrying about Cuddles.

spend twenty minutes with him at least twice a day. Once in the morning and once at night.

And I did. I brought my instructions with me, and twice a day I went through the list and ticked everything off. I did everything for Cuddles that I was supposed to. I did exactly what Mrs. Longaphy would have done if she'd been there. But there's a difference between somebody doing something because they want to and somebody doing something because they have to.

And that's what I mean about Mum's letters. Call me stupid, but they made me feel like Cuddles. Like I was number five on her to-do list or something. (1. Turn Bess into a responsible member of society. 2. Save endangered marine maggot from extinction. 3. Gather a dozen free-range eggs from cooperative chicken coop. 4. Clean fridge. 5. Write Telly so she knows we love her.)

And there was another thing. Mum never actually told me anything. Never told me what really happened. Never told me the good stuff. I mean, what exactly did Fern say about her husband and "other well-known members of the community"? Was Mum suggesting Grammie had a boyfriend? And my favorite: What did she mean by "spirited interactions" with Bess? Last time Bess had spirited interactions with someone they laid assault charges against her. I started to worry that Bess might have burnt down the house this time or locked Dad in the basement until he agreed to pay her way to Australia or something.

Why couldn't Mum just come out and tell me the truth? She probably thought she was doing the right thing—sparing me the gory details—but all she ended up doing was making me feel like I wasn't part of the family anymore. Like

I couldn't be trusted with the real story. She used code words when I was home too, but at least when I was there I could see what was really going on and decide for myself whether I wanted to crawl into Dreemland or not.

I guess it's not fair coming down on Mum like that. At least she wrote. Dad only sent me goofy postcards—the kind with a so-called unretouched photo of a fish wearing glasses, say, or a giant mosquito chasing a little tiny person down the beach. He'd scribble some stupid joke on the back like "I wondered where my specs went!" or "I heard there was a bad bug going around!" and then just filled the rest of the card with x's and o's.

I didn't mind. Dad's like me—not much of a talker. So it's not like I expected him to send me big long chatty letters all of a sudden. It did really bug me, though, when he sent me the same stupid fish card twice. I know Hemeon's Drugstore doesn't have many postcards to choose from, but he could have at least come up with a different joke. (It wasn't even all that funny the first time.)

As for Bess, she'd never written to me before. I was pretty sure it wasn't a good sign.

32

WHY AM i NOT SURPRiSED?

From: bess mercer<besslookinbabe@heatrash.com
To: Telly<telly@bitsieandbytesie.tv>
Subject: Urgent Parental Abuse

hey telly

sure is quiet since u left. u alwayz were such a party animal. hhok. having a wild time in the big city or what? let me no if u got n e body parts u want pierced. its about time u got something pierced. remember how many i used 2 have before the infection set in and dad did his big i'm a doctor thing and made me take them all out and stay in the hospital for a week? like whats he got against piercing? the guy doesn't appreciate the art form.

n e way I no a great place. they only take cash but they'll put a hole in anything! (n e thing u can stand that is. hhok.)

i love toronto. sure beats the crap out of B.M. i crashed there on my way 2 that nude square dancing workshop. the one that turned out 2 be the NEW square dancing workshop. remember how insane dad went? the guys a doctor and he acted as if he never saw a naked person before!!!!! he probably hasnt, nowing him. parents are soooo not normal.

like they wont even let me go n e where n e more! not even to the turkey burger for fries. dorothy says the police wont let me but i know its just her. i bet the "police" would let me go if it was organic. she wont even let me do n e thing. well, thats not true! how can i say that? she lets me read the paper (☺!!!!!) and go on line as long as its only to e-mail u (double ☺!!!!!!) is that fair? i steal one little bus and they act like i'm a criminal!!!!!

It was a really long letter so I'm not going to quote it word for word, but basically this is what else she said:

Me me me me me me me. Me me myself. I me me me me. Myself, I me me me. I I I I I me me I I. Me me memememe myself me. I me me me I. Etc. etc. etc.

I guess it was nice she took the time to write.

33
THE FACTS OF LIFE.

I got back to the studio during the coffee break. Zola was just getting Bitsie into a baby costume for the next scene. She'd tied a polka-dot ribbon in his hair and was pinning him into this humungous droopy diaper. Normally, I would have felt sorry for Bitsie, but not then. He deserved it. He was acting like a baby.

"So what was so urgent?" Zola asked me as she stuck in these big fake safety pins.

I forgot the e-mail was marked urgent. I had to laugh. Typical.

"Nothing," I said. "It's just my sister. She's the type that'll do anything for attention."

Bitsie looked right at me and mouthed the words, Just …like…you!

Did that ever make me mad! It wasn't even true. It was just stupid.

Zola was fumbling around, looking for a rattle, so she didn't notice Bitsie do anything. All she saw when she turned around was me leaning right into his face and hissing, "Jerk!"

I don't know what came over me. It was stupid. I was never that careless around other people. I mean, I knew what they'd say if I said, "It wasn't me who screamed/shoplifted/burped! It was the puppet!"

They'd say, "Telly, this isn't going to hurt. It will just make you sleep. When you wake up, you'll be in a special place where people can give you the help you need."

Anyway, Zola was staring at me with a, let's say, quizzical look on her face. This obviously required some explanation.

So I tried to laugh, but it sounded fake even to me. I went, "Ha-ha-ha-ha-ha. It's funny how puppets can look so human sometimes, isn't it? Like just then. Bitsie looked like such a jerk. It made me think he really was selfish and child-ish and ignorant and crude…"

I went on for a while like that—which was probably a mistake. Bitsie's face was completely blank. He looked about as human as an apple fritter—though not as cute. I could see Zola didn't get what was so jerky about him, but like I said, she was a really nice person and she always tried to see other people's points of view.

Or maybe she just wanted to stop me from ranting.

Whatever. Anyway, while she finished putting Bitsie's booties on, she started telling me about Arnold van Gurp, this puppet builder who claims his puppets are actually alive. Zola was just making conversation I knew, but to me it was way more than that. It was like someone casually blurting out, "Oh, did I mention that Uncle Roland is the real Santa Claus, and that's why he's always late for Christmas dinner?" It doesn't just change how you think about Uncle Roland—it changes your whole world.

My heart started beating like a rabbit's. I was thinking that this could be really important. This could be proof that I wasn't nuts after all.

Until Zola mentioned Arnold, I'd forgotten I used to feel crazy for believing Bitsie was real.

Okay, maybe I didn't really forget feeling crazy. Maybe I just didn't like admitting I was a nutcase. Or maybe I just preferred believing that I actually had a friend. A real one. Someone I could be myself with. Say anything I wanted to. It doesn't matter. All I'm saying is that for one reason or another I stopped asking myself if Bitsie was real.

But that doesn't mean the question wasn't still bouncing around in my head, waiting to be asked.

I made myself stop shaking. I tried to sound casual. I said, "You're kidding. There's no way that could be true or anything…I mean, live puppets? Ha-ha-ha-ha-ha."

Zola shrugged. "Some people say it's just a gimmick to sell his puppets," she said. "Other people think it's some form of mental illness. Arnold's been pretty cut off socially since he moved up to that little town. Beaconsfield? No. That's in Quebec. Bowserville? No. Something like that. Bousfield! That's it. It's way up north. Somewhere off the 404. It's very beautiful up there. Wild and not touristy. At least not yet…"

I was in no mood for a geography lesson. "But what do you think?" I tried to say it in a "dum-di-dum, whatever" kind of way.

"Me? Well, I guess I…"

Mel cut her off. Break was over. Bitsie had to get up on set. Like, right now!

I thought I was going to explode. I needed—I mean *needed*—to know what Zola thought!

As soon as she came back, I whispered, "You were saying …?" By now I wasn't doing a very good job of pretending this didn't matter to me. You know how dogs start wagging their tails and getting all drooly when their master is opening the Fido Beef Nuggets? Well, I wasn't quite that bad—but I was getting close.

"Saying what?" Zola whispered back. She wasn't really concentrating. She had to get Bytesie into his teenage brother gear.

"Is he crazy or isn't he?"

"Who? Arnold, you mean?"

In my head I was screaming, "Of course I mean Arnold!" but I just nodded, un-huh.

"Oh, I don't know," Zola said. "I used to work for him. He's not your run-of-the-mill TV executive—but Arnold's a good man. He's telling the truth—at least as he sees it. Everyone has the right to believe what they choose to believe. And we have to honor that belief—whether it resonates for us or not."

Just what I was afraid of.

Zola thought he was crazy too.

134

34

LIFE WAS SO MUCH EASIER IN DREEMLAND.

So Bitsie probably didn't exist. I guess I'd kind of suspected it all along. But that didn't stop me from being really mad at him that afternoon.

He kept on pulling his stupid stunts. He particularly liked breaking down in any way that made it look like Zola was to blame. I could have strangled him.

In the end, I didn't have to. Someone else got there first.

It was almost five—our usual quitting time—and we hadn't even got half the show taped. Everyone was really nervous. It wasn't our fault, but we all knew that we were in big trouble. Mel was going nuts at one of the cameramen, who may or may not have got the wrong shot, when the door to the studio opened and Kathleen came in. Mel immediately stopped screaming and patted the cameraman on the back like they were old buddies and that wasn't his spit dripping off the guy's glasses. It was really phony, but I didn't blame him for it. Nobody wanted to get Kathleen anymore wound up than she already was.

So we all put these fake "This-is-just-a-perfectly-normal-day" looks on our faces and started shooting again.

Everything went fine until Bitsie's line: "Friends are more precious than a sunshiny day!" I'd seen it coming and I knew it was going to be trouble. There was no way Bitsie would let a line that corny just slip by. But Jimmy read it perfectly, and Bitsie kept his lips in sync, and I started thinking that maybe even Bitsie was afraid of Kathleen.

Afraid of her? Yeah, right.

It didn't take me long to realize that to Bitsie this was like being asked to perform for the Queen or something. He finally had the audience he always dreamed of: Kathleen on the brink of insanity.

So like I was saying, Bitsie made it right to the end of the line perfectly—and then he did it. He rolled his eyes. Really sarcastic. Like 'Sunshiny day?' Oh, barf! Who writes this garbage?"

At first there was a little nervous titter of laughter from the studio. I mean, it *was* garbage.

Kathleen, of course, didn't titter. She just paced on the sidelines while Jimmy and Zola tried to figure out what was wrong with Bitsie's eye mec. Surprise, surprise. It seemed to be working perfectly.

So we shot the line again—and guess what?

Yup. Bitsie did it again. Four more times, in fact—and then Kathleen exploded.

Like "ka-boom!"

She started screaming. "What's the matter with that blankety-blank blank?"[52] Zola tried to say that she'd call Laird

---

[52] I'll leave the exact words to your imagination. Believe me, they were not what you'd expect to hear from someone who produces preschool television.

the puppet builder to come and fix him, but Kathleen just pushed her aside and charged up onto the set.

It was a weird scene. Kathleen was wearing one of those plain black suits that smart, successful people wear, but her face was completely crazy. Even her hair had gone kind of psycho. She didn't care. She just hurled herself screaming through the studio. She was so deranged that she missed the last step up to the set and fell flat on her face. One shoe flew off [53] and her skirt got all scrunched up around her waist. But that didn't slow her down. She just scrambled up onto one knee and lunged at Bitsie. She got him by the neck and started shaking him like she actually believed he was alive (but wished he wasn't).

Bitsie, of course, did this "innocent-bystander-attacked-by-raving-lunatic" thing. His eyes darted back and forth, his tongue hung out and his arms swung around like a rag doll's. I could tell other people were falling for it. They looked really upset to see this helpless little latex alien at the mercy of an obviously demented producer. It made me feel sad. Nobody saw the other side of Kathleen—and after that little display I had the feeling that nobody was going to go looking for it.

Nick was the one who finally got things under control—which only made me love him more, of course. He ran up to the set and tried to pull Kathleen's skirt back down over her bum, but she kept swatting him away. To her, right then, the number of people who

---

[53] It beaned Mel in the head and I couldn't help noticing that the cameraman got a laugh out of that.

saw her underwear was completely beside the point. All she cared about was paying Bitsie back.

Nick knew better than to fight with her. He turned around and smiled at us like a principal at the end of a school concert and sort of half-screamed over her yelling and cursing. "Well, ha-ha. I think we've probably done about as much as we're going to today. Let's call it a wrap. We'll see you all back here Monday morning at seven. Have a good weekend!...Oh, Zola and Mel, I think Kathleen will probably want to have a word with you in her office now."

Frankly, I doubted it. Kathleen was still rolling around on the set with Bitsie, and personally, I would have just let her get it out of her system. I mean, by that point, what difference did it make? But I wasn't in charge. I tried to smile at Zola in an "it-won't-be-so-bad," way and she tried to smile back, but I knew she was upset. She was going to get it from Kathleen—and miss the bus to her boyfriend's concert too. I was glad I wasn't a grown-up.

Nick managed to pry Bitsie out of Kathleen's fist and talk her into pulling her skirt down, and the four of them headed off to the office. Everyone else was clearing out as fast as they could. Can you blame them? Nobody wanted to be next.

Bitsie was still lying on the set like a crime victim in a TV movie. Part of me felt like going up and rescuing him, but I decided against it. I wanted to know what I was going to say first. Do I tell him off—it was his fault after all—or do I try and comfort him? I knew Kathleen couldn't have hurt him—he's only latex—but it must have been pretty humiliating just the same.

I decided to put the puppet doubles away first. It would give me a chance to figure out what to do. I'd just come back from storing Rom and Ram and was leaning toward giving Bitsie a piece of my mind when Zola walked in.

Or rather ran in.

I was surprised she was back so soon. I figured Kathleen must have just come straight out and fired her.

"What happened?" I asked. "What did Kathleen say?"

Zola was zooming around like the Roadrunner on fast-forward. Cleaning the work table, dusting the puppets and practically throwing them into the storage room. "She didn't say a thing."

I was relieved.

For a second, that is, until Zola added, "She just cried. Sobbed, in fact. Nick finally just let us go. It was horrible." She shook her head in that sad way people on the news do when the reporter asks them what it feels like to watch their favorite cow get carried away by a tornado or something. I got the feeling Zola would have nightmares about this for the rest of her life.

"I'm trying not to think about it," she said, going back to throwing stuff in drawers. "If I leave right now, I can catch the bus to Jacob's concert. He'll help me. He used to volunteer in a psychiatric hospital before he became a musician, so he'll understand."

Well, it looked at least like something good was going to come out of this mess.

Zola tossed a few of those guinea pig treats she likes into her bag, kissed me on the cheek and bolted.

She was practically out the door before she realized it. "Oh! I forgot Bitsie!" I shooed her away.

"Run! Run! I'll deal with him!"

"But I have to call Laird about fixing his eye mec too! I better stay."

I slung her bag back over her shoulder and pushed her out the door.

"Go!" I said. "I can handle Bitsie. It'll be easy."

Ha!

I've never been so wrong about anything in my life.

35

THE GUY WAS A MANIAC.

Zola was gone like a minute when I turned around and saw Bitsie standing on the set sticking a big sharp utility knife into the side of his head. I tried to act as if that was perfectly normal.

"All right, Bitsie. Drop the weapon and let's go beddy-bye."

He glared at me and poked the knife in farther.

"Put me in that storage closet and I'll tear the back of my head off!" The guy clearly had been watching too many late-night movies.

I had no idea what he was talking about, but I really wasn't in the mood for another one of Bitsie's stupid stunts. I went to grab the knife, but I forgot how fast he was. I pretended I didn't care.

"Fine. It's your head."

Bitsie was ready for that. "Yeah, but you're the one who's supposed to be putting me away. And Zola's the one who'll get in trouble if anything happens to me."

These were both good points, but I still didn't know where he was going with them.

"What am I supposed to do with you if I don't put you in the storage closet? Take you to the mall? Ha! I don't think so."

Bitsie sighed like we'd been through this a thousand times. "No, not the mall." Big eye roll. "You're taking me to Arnold van Gurp's!"

36
THE END OF THE WORLD
AS I KNEW IT.

Of course. Bitsie'd been listening to Zola too!

Who could blame him for wanting to meet Arnold? It must have been like thinking you're an orphan all your life and then hearing there's a man who looks just like you living three streets away. Of course you'd want to find out if you were related. It made perfect sense. But there was an obvious problem.

"You tear off the back of your head," I said, "and Zola gets in trouble. You run away, and Zola gets in trouble. It's all the same to me. Why should I take you there?" I was still being tough because Bitsie had put me through too much to just give in to him that easily.

Bitsie didn't put the knife down, but something about his eyes changed. "If I stay here with only half a head," he said, "both Zola and I will be miserable. You take me to van Gurp's and at least one of us will be happy."

He was right, but that didn't make it any easier for me. Who was I going to hurt? My best friend who could also be a big selfish jerk? Or the nicest person I ever knew?

I didn't have time to decide. The door to the studio opened, and Bitsie and I both dived under the set.

It was Nick. Looking for something.

"I don't see it here, Kathleen."

She didn't answer. Unless you call a big wet sob an answer.

"But that's all right." Nick was so nice. His voice was all soft and I'll-take-care-of-you. "I don't think you'll be using your cell phone this weekend."

More sobs.

"Now, now, now. I know that sounds painful to you at the moment, but it might turn out to be a good thing. You need a break."

That really set her off.

"I do need a break!" Kathleen started burbling away like a little kid having a tantrum. "It's not fair! All this stress! The money problems! The puppet problems!"

She had a real big boo-hoo about that and I glared at Bitsie. He just sat there, of course, scraping the latex from the inside of his ear with the utility knife and acting like Kathleen was talking about Big Bird's lisp or something.

Nick was saying, "I know, I know," and leading her out the door.

"And if that's not bad enough," Kathleen really spat this out, "I get saddled with Dodo's kid for the whole summer!"

Right then, everything in the world changed for me.

Nick said, "You're right. That was an awful lot to ask you to do," and closed the door.

I turned to Bitsie and said, "When's the first bus to Bousfield?"

37
SOMEONE OLDER AND WISER.

I couldn't cry in front of Bitsie. I had to make myself busy. Get my brain so full that it didn't have room for Kathleen or Nick or all the other bad thoughts that were just dying to get in there and break my heart.

I got on the phone. The only bus to Bousfield that weekend left at 7 a.m. Saturday and cost $79, round trip. Bitsie was thrilled. He figured we could just crash in front of the TV that night, then head off bright and early for the bus station the next morning.

"How do you expect us to pay for the ticket?" I said in that "you idiot" voice he liked to use with me. "I spent all my emergency money on must-have items like glow-in-the-dark dog collars and leopard skin bras! I'm broke."

Bitsie tried to look sheepish. I ignored him and just focused on the problem. We didn't have many options. Use my taxi vouchers? I was mad at Kathleen but still didn't think it was fair to charge her thousands of dollars for a cab ride to Bousfield. Yard sale? No time, and I doubted there was much of a market for secondhand bras anyway. Borrow the money? Yeah, right. From whom? Steal it? No way. I was in enough trouble already.

I wished there were someone I could ask—but who? Who would know what to do in a mess like this?

Of course.

Bess.

38

From: Telly<telly@bitsieandbytesie.tv>
To: bess mercer<besslookinbabe@heatrash.com>
Subject: Urgent Transportation

Dear Bess,

It was so nice to get your long newsy letter. Oh and it brought back some memories! That crazy trip of yours to the Nude Square Dancing Convention! Ha-ha. That must have been quite an adventure! Funny thing is, I can't for the life of me remember how you got there. I don't recall any criminal charges being laid so I figure you didn't steal a credit card or hi-jack a car. So how did you get there? It's silly, but I don't think I'll be able to sleep until I find out. It's sort of like having a song go round and round in your head, but you can't remember the words. So annoying.

Please get back to me as soon as humanly possible with the information. If I get it tonight, I promise I'll write Mum Monday and ask her to let you go to the Turkey Burger again.

Desperately,

Telly

From: bess mercer<besslookinbabe@heatrash.com>
To: Telly<telly@bitsieandbytesie.tv>
Subject: Urgent Transportation

u mean it about the turkey burger?

From: Telly<telly@bitsieandbytesie.tv>
To: bess mercer<besslookinbabe@heatrash.com>
Subject: Urgent Transportation

Yes.

From: bess mercer<besslookinbabe@heatrash.com>
To: Telly<telly@bitsieandbytesie.tv>
Subject: Urgent Transportation

its a deal. i hitched 2 halifax and then busked on spring
garden road. i sang oops i did it again 4 about 5 hours
straight and then the guy who owned the store i was
standing in front of gave me $173 2 leave. i was sort of
insulted because i was getting pretty good. i even made
up some of my own verses. but who cares? i got enuf for
a bus ticket 2 TO.

looking forward 2 that burger. B

39
GOOD IDEAS COME FROM
THE STRANGEST PLACES.

Hitchhiking. I couldn't do that. I'd be too scared.

Busking. I couldn't do that either. I'd be even more scared. Bess was the type who'd just open her mouth and wail away, and it wouldn't matter to her how bad she was as long as people kept throwing money in her hat.

There was no way I could put anyone through that, and I told Bitsie so.

"Who said you had to sing?" he said.

"Well, what else can I do? People are hardly going to give me money for reciting the times table." Which is about the only thing I was ever very good at.

"No—but people would give you money for puppeteering!"

I was just about to say I couldn't do that either when I realized I didn't have to. For once, Bitsie'd had a good idea.

40
IT WENT TO HIS HEAD...

We were lucky. It was June and warm. There were plenty of people on the sidewalks that night, just strolling around. I found a good place on Yonge Street near an ice-cream stand and took Bitsie out of my knapsack. Only he didn't look like Bitsie very much anymore. Just to be on the safe side, we'd borrowed some things from the costume department and disguised him as a girl.

A very ugly girl. With big red felt lips, glasses, a kerchief with orange braids sticking out, and a peasant blouse with two tennis balls glued underneath in the appropriate places. I thought he was going to hate it, but he was so flattered by the idea that some-one might recognize him that he was practically unbearable.[54]

I told myself this was going to be easy. All I had to do was move my lips as if I was trying not to move my lips and just let Bitsie do the rest. I put out a hat we'd also borrowed from the costume department and got started.

---

[54] The guy was an egomaniac. You'd think if they could put a man on the moon, someone would be able to invent latex that wasn't so full of itself.

It was easy. Really easy. Bitsie was so into it. He went nuts. He did the Macarena. He did impressions of Nelly Furtado and the prime minister and some famous lady who used to get married all the time. He sang goofy fake opera songs and made jokes that I didn't get.

But I guess they were funny. We'd only been doing it for about five minutes, but we already had a big crowd— and they were all laughing their heads off. Bitsie loved it. I should have too, I guess. Our hat was filling up pretty fast. But something was making me nervous.

We were too good.

We were attracting too much attention.

I tried to tone Bitsie down a bit—but what could I do? I couldn't say anything because people would get suspicious if we were both talking at the same time (and believe me, Bitsie had no intention of shutting up). I couldn't stop him from moving. He was in charge there too. So I threw my hoodie over his head thinking I'd say, "That's all for now, folks," and they'd leave and I'd have a chance to talk to him alone about my worries. But that didn't work either. Bitsie just threw the hoodie off, made some joke about puppet abuse and picked up right where he left off.

I tried to relax and go with it. I figured we almost had enough money so we wouldn't have to do it much longer.

I was almost calm—until the lady with the yellow hair asked me that question.

"Where did a young girl like you learn to puppeteer like this?"

Of course I didn't get to answer it. Bitsie took it upon himself to supply all the gory details. He started out okay.

He said, "Mostly I just taught myself. I've always been interested in theater and comedy."

That would have been fine if he'd just left it at that. But he had everybody's attention, and he was hardly going to waste it.

He lowered his eyes as if this was tough for him to talk about and went on. "Puppeteering became a way for me to escape the horrors of my family life. I retreated into my imaginary world in order to forget the physical and emotional abuse that awaited me at the hands of my cruel stepfather…"

Do I need to continue—or did you see that episode of *Crime Wave* too? Unfortunately, nobody in the crowd seemed to have. They all got these really sad looks on their faces and started throwing more money in the hat. Bitsie, I could just tell, thought he was brilliant. He started adding things that weren't even in the TV show. About how I was living on the street now. About how my stepfather had a contract out on me. About how I'd started to believe that my puppet was talking to me. Things like that.

The lady, who by this time had mascara streaming down her face, touched me on the shoulder. She said, "Wait here. I know someone who can help you. A policewoman who's dealt with this type of thing before." Then she ran off to get the cops.

Was Bitsie worried that the law was now on our trail? Ha! It didn't even cross his mind. He was busy talking to a reporter from the *National Herald*, who'd noticed all the people and wanted to do a story on us for the next day's paper.

That's all I needed to hear. I grabbed Bitsie, my knapsack and the hat and bolted through the crowd.

Was Bitsie ever pissed off! He was screaming, "Hey! I was talking to that guy!" and everybody, I'm sure, was thinking what an amazing performer I was to be able to run and puppeteer backwards over my shoulder at the same time. Luckily, they all thought the escape was part of the act so it took a while before anyone started running after us.

There was no way I was going to stop until we were miles away from all those people and that reporter's flashing camera. I didn't even slow down when Bitsie started biting my ear.

41
SOMETHING TO REMEMBER.

"You only have $78.37 here." The guy at the bus station wasn't going to let us go to Bousfield because we were sixty-three cents short. I couldn't believe it!

Normally, I would have just apologized for wasting his time and walked away. I mean, I was hardly the type to argue with people. I was hardly the type to even talk to people.

But this time was different. Maybe it was because I was desperate. Or maybe it was because I was disguised. Wearing those pink glasses of Bitsie's and that stupid kerchief, I didn't look like me anymore.[55] I guess I didn't feel like me anymore either.

I said, "I know we're short. I mean, I'm short. But I did have enough money—honest. It's just that I fell when I was running to get here. See?"

I lifted my leg way up to the counter so he could see the hole in my pants and my bloody knee.

"And I was bleeding really badly so I had to use some of my bus money for Band-Aids."

---

[55] And I was hoping that none of those people who had been running after us would think so either.

By now, he wasn't even looking at me. He was busy filling out some form and I thought, How rude! But I didn't let it show.

I just kept going. "I had to use the whole box. It was that bad! I was even getting a little light in the head. Probably because I lost so much blood. Or maybe just because it was so gross. It really was terrible."

He looked at me and sighed and pushed the form he'd been filling out across the counter.

"One round-trip ticket to Bousfield. That'll be $78.37. I'll take the sixty-three cents out of my donut money."

"Oh, thank you, thank you, thank you!" I started squealing like I'd just guessed how much the do-it-yourself face-lift kit cost on *The Price is Right*.

"No, thank *you*," he said, patting his belly and smiling for the first time. "It'll do me good to have one less sour-cream old-fashioned. Next!"

Giving up a donut for a complete stranger! People are so nice. Sometimes it's easy to forget that.

42

NOW SHOWING AT A
BRAIN NEAR YOU.

We spent the night in the bus station. I was tired and hungry and scared. The donut man had gone home for the night. Everyone still there looked mean or crazy or both. The fact that I thought the donut man was mean at first too didn't make me feel any better at three in the morning. I wouldn't have had a wink of sleep except that Bitsie was desperate to keep me happy. He was worried I was going to take him back to the studio. I'm sure that's the only reason he volunteered to stand guard.

Or rather lie guard. I put my knapsack on the bench so Bitsie could see out the hole at the top. Then I put my head on the knapsack and fell asleep.

It's funny how you say "fall asleep," because that's not usually what happens. How often do you "fall"? Usually you just sort of float asleep. Like you're on an air mattress or something, just drifting. One minute you're in the shallow waters of Wakey-Wakey Beach; then, without even knowing it, you've floated out into the wide-open seas of the Slumber Strait.[56]

---

[56] Okay, I admit it. That wasn't my idea. I stole it from "Bytesie Goes Beddy-bye." It was as stupid as most of the episodes, but I thought Audrey had a point about that falling asleep thing.

But that night I fell asleep, and I must have knocked myself out when I hit bottom because I didn't move again until 6:55 when this really loud announcement came on. "All passengers should now be on board for the 7:03 bus to Neewack, Goldrink, New Cumberland, Bousfield and Lower Shinimicas."

I unstuck my tongue from the roof of my mouth, grabbed my knapsack and stumbled onto the bus half-awake. I was sort of glad I was feeling so terrible. When you need a toothbrush as badly as I did, it's easy to keep your mind off your other problems. The back of the bus was empty so I put the knapsack against the armrest and stretched out over three seats. I was hoping to just fall asleep again. Hard—the way I did before—so that nothing could start worming around in my brain until I woke up in Bousfield.

158

Like Bitsie was going to let that happen.

He started yammering away about all the things he and Arnold's puppets were going to do together. It was going to be so much fun after being cooped up with those foam-heads all these years. I couldn't blame him for being excited, but that doesn't mean I had to listen to him. The less I thought about what we were doing, the better. I closed the top of the knapsack to shut out his voice and tried to go to sleep.

He pulled open the side pocket and started talking about how he hoped they had cable up in Bousfield so he and the boys (as he called his soon-to-be new friends) could get the Sports Channel.

I stuffed the fake braids on my kerchief into my ears and rolled over and tried again. But it was too late. I wasn't going to be able to fall asleep anymore. I lay there staring at the grey-carpeted ceiling of the bus and tried not to listen as my "pillow" yakked on and on about puppet movie theaters and puppet bowling alleys and puppet malls and all the wonderful things he was pretty sure he'd find in beautiful downtown Bousfield.

I didn't know how I was going to survive a six-hour bus trip with old Motormouth blabbing away.

Then my head went all quiet inside, and Bitsie's voice disappeared. I hadn't zoned out like that in a long time. Not since Bess stole that bus back in Beach Meadows and it looked like we'd all end up in a ditch or Mexico or something.

Do you know what the funny thing was this time? When I wanted to blank out all the scary things that were happening right then, guess what I thought of.

Bess—stealing the bus. Suddenly, it didn't seem so terrible. It seemed kind of, I don't know, "charming," as my mother would say. I thought about Bess gunning down Sow's Ear Road just the way it happened, but without feeling afraid of crashing or afraid of what the Mounties were going to do or afraid of the look on my mother's face when we finally stopped. I thought about Bess singing that stupid song, which didn't seem so stupid anymore, and her making Alyssa feel like a star just because of her bright pink throw-up.

For the next six hours I was glued to my own little mental movie, "Me and My Crazy Sister," starring the zany but loveable Bess Mercer. The stealing, the lying, the broken windows all started to seem like the good old days.

Maybe that's part of growing up. Have you noticed old people always think that way? Everything that happened before—no matter how horrible it must have been at the time—is better than whatever's happening right now. That's why Grammie gets all dreamy-eyed talking about the war,

159

I guess. Or why Kathleen loves telling stories about being poor as a kid and eating secondhand Queenburgers and having the heat so low that she had to wear her snowsuit to bed every night. You'd almost think someone forced her to give it all up for a fancy condo, expensive clothes and Apricot-Kiwi Emulsion.

I wasn't thinking all that, of course. I was just enjoying the movie. Every so often a little thought would creep in that didn't fit. Mum crying, say. Or Dad looking out the window at nothing. Or the sound of the social worker dropping Bess's big, fat file on the kitchen table. When that happened the movie would click right off as if someone—probably Bess—had switched the channel to some gross thing like I *Want You Dead* or *Abdominal Surgery* or even one of those ads about starving babies. It's hard to pretend life's just grand when you're watching a kid die or someone get their liver yanked out.

But I'd just grab the remote back—not the real remote, but you know what I mean—and start watching the Bess movie again. I chuckled when she locked the principal out of his office and sang dirty songs over the PA system until the janitor knocked the door down. I smiled at her giving me a shirt for Christmas that just so happened to be her size, not mine. I even had one of those little happy cries over the beautiful Remembrance Day speech she gave about our grandfather's heroic war service, and this time it didn't bother me a bit that our grandfather had flat feet and never went to war.

It didn't matter. The stories did what they had to.

They got me to Bousfield without thinking how stupid I was for ruining my life.

160

43
THE GREAT VAN GURP.

The man at the gas station gave us directions to Arnold van Gurp's and said we couldn't miss it. At first I thought that was because Bousfield was so small. The correct word for it, I think, is puny. Just the Petrocan where the bus dropped us, a video store that also sells pizza and picks up your dry-cleaning, and a bunch of houses.

But the way the gas station guy laughed when he said, "You can't miss it!" and the way the lady getting her tank filled laughed even louder got me worried. I can't say exactly why, but it did. They say you're supposed to follow your instincts, and my instincts right then were saying, "Stop. Go home. It's not too late to turn around." But the puppet in my knapsack was saying, "Would you hurry up?" and poking me really hard in the ribs, and that voice in my head was sobbing, "I get saddled with Dodo's kid," so what could I do? I started walking to Arnold van Gurp's.

I turned down Bousfield's one and only side street and headed for the very end. Along the way, there were two old people sitting on one of those big wooden swings, but otherwise the road was deserted.[57] I started whispering into the knapsack. I reminded Bitsie that he was supposed to play dumb and let me do the talking until I figured out what kind of guy this Arnold was. I made it sound like I was doing it for Bitsie—like I just wanted to make sure I was giving him to a good home—but who was I kidding? I was doing it for me. I didn't want Arnold to think I was nuts until I knew that he was nuts too. I wanted his puppets to talk first.

The houses seemed to end, and I was starting to think the gas station guy had laughed because he was playing a joke on me, when I saw something pink peeking through the trees. As I got closer, I caught glimpses of bright yellow and blue too, and bit by bit I began to realize there was a house back there.

A cartoon house.

A kind of shabby run-down cartoon house.

It looked like someone let a five-year-old design it. It was sort of skinny at the bottom and fat at the top. The roof was orange and curled up at the sides. The chimney leaned over one way and the front door leaned over the other way. The windows had those big black crosses in the middle just like they do in little kids' drawings. And in case I had any doubt if I had the right place, there was a giant red cartoon mailbox with the yellow words "van gurp."

I guess the gas station guy was right. You couldn't miss it.

I rang the big purple doorbell, and this loud rinky-dink version of "The Lollipop Song" started to play. Bitsie groaned—he hates that kind of stuff—and I was just

162

---

[57] All out picking up their dry-cleaning at the video store, I guess.

shushing him when the door opened and Arnold van Gurp said, "Yes??"

He looked odd. Not as odd as his house but pretty darn weird. He was about five foot nothing. His yellow hair was all slicked down perfectly and his teeth stuck out over his bottom lip even when his mouth was closed. He was dressed in a business suit, just like my dad would wear, only Arnold's was bright orange and his shirt was green and his tie was pink-and-yellow striped. I figured he must have really liked hot dogs too, because over the three weeks he must have been wearing those same clothes he'd collected quite a large number of ketchup stains.

It was a pretty weird outfit for anyone, let alone a guy as old as Mel.

Not that I could talk. I was still wearing that lame disguise—Bitsie's pink glasses and the kerchief with the fake braids—so I must have looked kind of strange myself. Maybe that's why Arnold seemed to like me right away. I mean, it looked like we were related—or at least shopped at the same stores.

"Now, who might you be, and what's brought you here to Chateau van Gurp?" he said, all cheery like he was hosting a game show or something. Everything about the guy made me think he'd spent way too much time in kids' TV.

"Hi. I'm…"

I had to stop right there. Somehow it didn't seem like a good idea to give my real name.

"I'm…well, I'm a budding puppeteer!"

"You don't say! And so you've made the long and treacherous pilgrimage to far-off Bousfield to visit the Great van Gurp. Well, I'm flattered! Come in! Come in!"

He pulled the door open and bowed, and I stepped into a living room that was exactly what you'd expect after seeing the outside of the house. I was still sort of hoping to see a room full of puppets, all watching TV or playing video games or just doing stuff to bug each other. I was still hoping that this would turn out to be the home Bitsie always wanted.

And there were puppets everywhere, but they weren't what you'd call a very lively bunch. They were just draped over the big lopsided furniture like rag dolls. I tried not to jump to conclusions. I wasn't letting Arnold see the real Bitsie yet. Why should he let me see the real side of his puppets?

I understood that—but I couldn't let him stall forever. I wanted to catch the 8 p.m bus back to Toronto so I could enjoy my last day of freedom before I was sent to jail for the rest of my life.

I decided to give Arnold a chance to feel comfortable with me before I popped the question. I said, "What a lovely home. So are your puppets alive or aren't they?" which didn't come out as smoothly as I hoped it would.

"Oh! So word has gotten out!" he said. He tried to look all modest and everything, but I could tell he was thrilled. "Why, yes, every van Gurp creation comes with a free gift. The gift of life!!!!!" He threw his arms up in the air like he was a gymnast who'd just won gold at the Oddball Olympics or something, and I guess I should have clapped, but I just stood there staring at him until he put his arms back down, all casual, like he'd just been having a little stretch or something and said, "Would you like to meet my puppet friends? Stay for tea and cookies, perhaps?"

Cookies! I was so hungry. I said I'd love to.

He led me into the kitchen and introduced me to the three puppets sitting at the big green table. Mingo the Monkey: Caleb the Cowboy and Princess Peachy.

I'd like to say that they all jumped up to shake my hand, but they didn't. They just sat there with their big heads kind of hanging over the back of their chairs and their mouths open.

This didn't seem to bother Arnold at all. He said, "Oh, they're playing shy again! Sometimes they get that way with strangers."

He told me to sit down, and then he crawled around on the floor until he was kneeling behind the puppets. He put one arm around Mingo's shoulder and whispered to him, "It's okay. I know for a fact this young lady loves monkeys!" Arnold made a big show of kissing Mingo's cheek and patting his fuzzy head. I guess he was hoping I wouldn't notice his other hand trying to wiggle its way up the back of Caleb's shirt.

That's all I had to see to know the guy was a fake. Fake as the plastic cookies he had sitting on the table for tea.[58]

I put one of those "how cute!" smiles on my face and started looking for the right time to say "It's been lovely meeting you, but I really must dash."

"Caleb" was just saying, "Why, heck, Mingo, you ole flea-bitten varmint! Don't you like your new lady friend?"

Mingo didn't have a chance to answer.

"Ah, forget about her!" Bitsy yelled as he wiggled out of my knapsack. "You're going to *love* me!"

---

[58] Boy was that a heart breaker. I kind of always suspected Arnold, but I at least figured I'd get real cookies.

44
YOU'D THINK HE'D HAVE NOTICED.

"Hey! Don't look so shocked!" Bitsie was saying to Mingo and Princess Peachy. I guess the blank expression on their faces could look like surprise if you really wanted it to. "You think you're the only living puppets around?…Ha! Think again, folks!" He loved knowing stuff other people didn't.

Bitsie did a little cha-cha-cha dance on top of the table. I should have just grabbed him and stuffed him back into my knapsack and hoped that Arnold was thinking about something else and hadn't noticed anything unusual. But I didn't. I was still trying to get my brain in gear.

Arnold, by this time, had, like, staggered back up onto his feet. His face was white and Caleb was still hanging upside down off one hand. Arnold gawked at Bitsie, closed his eyes, shook his head, then gawked at him again. It didn't help. The puppet was still dancing and talking all by itself.

Arnold looked at me all crazy-eyed and went, "How do you do that?"

Bitsie, I guess, thought Arnold was talking to him. "The cha-cha?" he said. "Oh, please! It's easy! It's just one-two-cha-cha-cha. One-two-cha-cha-cha! C'mon! Just follow old Bitsie! That's it! Right foot first, then left. Atta-boy! Put some hip movement into it, Arnie! Yeah!"

It was probably just because he was so shocked, but Arnold actually started following Bitsie's cha-cha steps. He wasn't bad either. He even seemed to catch on pretty fast to the turns and arm movements Bitsie'd thrown in. But I could tell by Arnold's wide-open mouth and shifty eyes that he was still thinking of something else.

Bitsie, of course, didn't notice anything. He was in puppet heaven!

"C'mon, you guys! Isn't anyone else here going to dance?" Bitsie gave Princess Peachy a friendly little nudge with his foot and she fell out of her chair and landed flat on her face.

That was the first time I ever saw Bitsie scared. He went, "Sorry, Arnie...I mean, Mr. van Gurp!" in this really chicken voice. He jumped down off the table, threw Princess Peachy into a fireman's hold and got her back into her seat.

"How's that, Highness? All better or what?" She didn't answer. Bitsie looked back and forth between me, the Princess and Arnold. I thought he must have figured it out by now, and as crazy as this sounds, I was sort of hoping he'd know what to do. I sure didn't.

Arnold, meanwhile, had pulled himself together. His face had gotten a little pink again and he sort of smiled. He was watching Bitsie's every move, like he was looking for strings or something and not seeing any. He was getting ideas.

"Oh, don't worry about her, Bitsie," he said in this really fake voice. "The Princess was up very late last night!"

Oh, c'mon. How lame was that?

Not lame enough. Bitsie fell for it.

He went, "*She* was? Ha! I was up *all* night! I kid you not! We ran away from the studio yesterday and had to camp out at the bus station."

"Oh, really?" Arnold was very interested.

"Really," Bitsie said. "I wish you'd been there. It was so cool. Disguises—the whole bit! It was like *Spy International: The Series*. Only better. No one could find out who we were or where we were going. Ab-so-lute-ly top-secret."

Arnold was practically rubbing his hands together the way the bad guys do in old cartoons.

"Really?" he said. "So no one knows you're here…"

"Not a soul! As you can see, we made sure no one would ever be able to identify my lovely sidekick here as the plain, mousy Tel…"

"Bit-sieeee!" I screamed. I held the "-sie!" part for a while so my brain could figure out what to say next. "These cheap robots!" I kind of whispered to Arnold. "I had some trouble with his software program. Sometimes he says crazy things!"

Arnold would have gone for the computer story, I'm sure of it, if Bitsie had just kept his mouth shut.

"*I* say crazy things?!?" he went, all indignant. "Listen to her!"

Bitsie bent over and did that look-up-my-bum thing. "Do you see a computer there?"

Arnold did a very thorough inspection. I guess he wanted to be extra sure he was seeing what he thought he was seeing.

"No, I can't," he said and looked at me in a creepy way. "Nothing at all. Just the standard mecs."

Bitsie snorted. "Ignore them! They're just for show."

Arnold smiled. A big, happy smile that made me feel sick to my stomach.

"So, you like to dance, do you, Bitsie?" he said.

"Ooooh, yes!" Bitsie did a little hip-hop rapper move with his hands and neck.

"Then you *have* to meet these other pals of mine!" Suddenly, Arnold was Mr. Hospitality again. "They're just down the hall."

Warning sirens went off in my head. I went to grab Bitsie and bolt with him, but Arnold was faster.

"Here, I'll give you a ride!" he said and tossed Bitsie up onto his shoulder like he was the nicest dad at the class party or something. What could I do? I snatched my knapsack and followed. I tried to catch Bitsie's eye, but when I did he just gave me a big thumbs-up sign.

Arnold took us down the hall. He unlocked a door at the end and showed us in. It was a tall room with one tiny window way up high, but it was full of puppets all stacked on top of each other like firewood. I figured Bitsie had to understand what was going on now. People don't usually stack their "friends" in locked rooms. At least where I come from.

But I guess it's like Grammie always says. We all believe what we want to believe.

Bitsie said, "Boy, these guys look like they were up late too!" and crawled down off Arnold's shoulder. "I am going to like it here! Par-ty Central! This is definitely my kind of place!"

He noticed something and stopped yakking mid-boogie. "Hey! Isn't that Mavor the Mammoth?" He trotted over to a pile of fur in the far corner of the room. "From *Prehistoric Preschool?* . . . It is! Whaddya know!"

I heard a click. I turned around. Arnold had left the room. I heard another noise and knew right away what it was.

Arnold had locked the door.

170

45

A LITTLE DEMONSTRATION.

"I had no idea you were alive!" Bitsie was saying to this dusty brown furball with one missing eye. "Had I known, I would have called you when your show got cancelled."

I couldn't believe it. Was Bitsie blind? The only thing that would have made Mavor the Mammoth look any less alive was to have an axe in his head and some flies buzzing around the wound.

"Bitsie," I said.

He ignored me. It was like when Kayleigh Mombourquette, my so-called best friend in Grade Two, met Melissa Weagle. I didn't count anymore. Bitsie had new friends to talk to now. "It wasn't your fault," he was saying. "You didn't have much to work with. I mean, a dinosaur day care? Whose idea was that? Don't these people realize that there's not a mammoth alive who could fit in those eensy-teensy chairs?" Bitsie rolled his eyes and elbowed Mavor in that old "Can-you-believe-these-guys?" way. Mavor's front leg bent up backwards and landed in his ear. It stayed there.

I tried again. "Bitsie."

Bitsie turned and looked at me like he was Mr. Rhodenizer and I'd just horked a spitball at the chalkboard or something.

He got all prissy with me. "You had all day to talk to me on the bus, but you chose not to. Now, if you don't mind, I'm getting acquainted with a colleague of mine…So, Mavor, after *Prehistoric Preschool*…"

This was hopeless.

I rattled the doorknob. I pounded on the door. I threw myself against it. Bitsie shook his head like I was a hyperactive three-year-old and ignored me. Again.

He would have kept on ignoring me too, but then Arnold—his new idol—rapped on the other side of the door.

"Calm down now," Arnold said in a reasonably nice way. "I'm not going to hurt you. I just don't want you going anywhere."

Bitsie laughed. "Arnie, you don't have to worry about me! I'm here! I'm with you, man!"

I threw myself against the door again. Harder this time because my father's a doctor and, if I ever did manage to escape, I knew he'd be able to fix a broken collar bone.

Arnold and Bitsie were both screaming at me now to behave, and the door wasn't going anywhere, so I stopped and threw Mavor against the wall.

"Hey!" Bitsie went, all offended. "The guy just woke up! Would you give him a break?"

I grabbed a sailor and biffed him too. And a pink mouse. And a ladybug. And a walrus. And a panda ballerina. I'd just grab a leg and blast whatever was attached to it as hard as I could.

172

Bitsie was going, "Hey! Hey!" and "What are you doing?" and my favorite, "You're not making a very good first impression!" As if he'd know about making a good impression—first or otherwise.

Finally, I'd had it. My little demonstration wasn't working. I dropped the farmer I had by the overalls and waited until I heard Arnold walk away. "Bitsie," I whispered to him. "Can't you see? They're not alive! They're not asleep! These are just puppets! They're...foam-heads!"

Bitsie put his hands over Mavor's big floppy ears so he couldn't hear and glared at me. "You're just jealous!" he said. "Well, too bad. These are my friends and I'm staying here. I don't care what you say. So why don't you just go? Go home to your precious Kathleen and Mr. Dreeeeeeeeeeeeeeeeeeeeeeeeeamboat!"

173

"Fine," I said. "I think I will."

I went to open the door, all innocent. "Oh, gee, it seems to be locked. I wonder why that is. Maybe you could ask your good friend Arnie to let me out."

"I'd be delighted," Bitsie said, because of course we all know how perfect his manners are, and started calling for Arnold through the keyhole.

"Yes, Bitsie."

"Would you mind letting my former friend out please? It's time for her to go home." Bitsie looked at me in that "I-hope-I'm-making-myself-clear" way.

Arnold was apologetic. "Sorry, Bitsie," he said, "but I can't do that. I need her here to help with my next project."

Well, Bitsie thought that was the most hilarious thing he'd ever heard in his whole life! "Oh, please!" he went. "Her? Help? Ha! She's just a puppet wrangler, a *junior* puppet wrangler. She doesn't know anything. Nothing. Nada. Rien." He even said "rien" with a big wet French "r" like he was Celine Dion or Pepe Le Pew or somebody.[59]

There was silence from the other side of the door. For a second there, I thought Arnold was actually thinking of letting me go.

"Well, that may be true," he finally said, "but your friend still knows too much."

---

[59] I think that's what bugged me most of all. Don't you hate people who pretend they can speak French when they can't?

46

NOT THE SOLUTION I WOULD HAVE CHOSEN, BUT IT WORKED.

When it finally sunk in what was happening, Bitsie was furious. Way madder than I was. It was like he'd been betrayed or something.

He couldn't believe he fell for it. He pulled a puppet out of the stack and exploded. "Gary Gecko! No…no! It can't be true. I'm trapped in a room with the so-called star of *Library Lizards*'! He was acting like he thought he should have been on the double-A soccer team and instead got stuck playing with the girls under six. I got the feeling he wasn't upset about being locked up. He was upset about who he was locked up with. Typical Bitsie.

He yanked out another puppet. "Cleo-cat-ra!" he screamed and dropped it as if it was covered in kitty litter or something.

It was the same for every one of the puppets he looked at. Mr. Raging TV Addict knew them all. "Bathtub Buddies!—I'd rather hang out with shower scum. At least it has some personality!" "Math Mice—Get me the rat poison!" "Happy, Nappy, Pappy and Joe—or should I say Crappy, Crappy, Crappy and Schmoe?"

"Giggly Geese."

"Eartha and the Dirt Movers."

"Sinus and the Flu Bugs."

From what I could gather, it was like every puppet from every crummy cancelled show ever made was stuffed there in that room.

My guess was Arnold hadn't had much luck in the television game, and it dawned on me that Bitsie would look pretty good to a desperate man. I wondered what Arnold would be ready to do for a hit series. I didn't want to stick around to find out. That orange suit of his was enough to convince me that we were not dealing with a rational mind.

We had to get out of there.

I needed a plan.

I looked around. There was the door that I'd already tried. There was one of those vent things in the floor that was too little even for Bitsie to get through. And there was the window.

It was high up and it was small but it was our only hope. I stacked Mavor, Gary, Eartha and Cleo-cat-ra on top of each other and climbed up. The crunching sound was pretty gross, but it got me where I had to go. I could just reach the ledge. The window must have been painted shut when Arnold could still afford paint because it wasn't moving. I picked and I pried and I broke all my nails, and after a really long time I managed to slide it open about ten centimeters.

The squeak of the window actually made Bitsie look up. He was so busy screaming at Bradley Broccoli for having the nerve to make a kids' show about vegetables that he hadn't even noticed what I was doing until then.

"Hey! Good idea!" he said.

Here Bitsie was finally giving me a compliment and I had to tell him to shut up. I didn't want Arnold to get suspicious.

I climbed back down and whispered to Bitsie as fast as I could. "You've got to get out this window, sneak in the house, open the door and get me out." Okay, so it was a little short on details, but it was a plan. And anyway, Bitsie hardly needed tips from me on sneaking around. He was the expert at it.

I made Bitsie a rope out of tied-together puppet clothes and attached it to his waist. He was going to need it to get down to the ground. Then I picked him up and was about to shove him through the window when I heard Arnold coming.

"Excuse me," he said. "Why so quiet in there all of a sudden?"

"I'm putting Bitsie to sleep," I said. "He was up really late last night." I figured if it worked for Arnold, it would work for me.

And can you believe it? He swallowed it. His own stupid excuse!

"Oh. Okay. Good," he went. "Bitsie's going to need his energy. I've got a big day planned for him tomorrow."

I bet he did.

I waited until I heard Arnold leave, then I stepped back up on Cleo-cat-ra and shoved Bitsie through the window.

Or at least I tried to. No matter which way I pushed him, his beak stopped us every time. "You're going to have to squish me," he whispered.

I know this sounds really terrible because it's easy to forget that he doesn't feel anything, but I put Bitsie on the floor and walked back and forth across his head. I even jumped a bit on the beaky part.

It was no good. His eyes seemed a bit farther apart and his head seemed a little squarer than before, but that beak of his was still not going to go through the window.

I sat down to think. I closed my eyes and rubbed my forehead. How was I going to get Bitsie out of there?

I heard a weird, blubbery sound and I opened my eyes. Bitsie had torn his beak off.

"Okay," he whispered. "Let's try it again."

47

SOME ADDED COMPLICATIONS.

Bitsie slipped through the window fine and landed on the ground. Now all I had to do was wait.

What if Arnold came back and found him gone? What if Arnold caught him in the house? What if Bitsie just made a run for it and left me there on my own? What would Kathleen do when she saw Bitsie's nose job? I had a lot of things to think about so I wasn't bored.

I was so weirded out by all the bad stuff that was going to happen that I barely noticed when a phone started ringing.

It took me a few seconds to realize it was in the room with me somewhere. If I had a phone, I had some options. I started throwing things around like a crazy person, looking for it. Where was it coming from? I stopped panicking and followed the sound.

To my knapsack. I couldn't believe it.

I scrambled around inside and pulled out—Kathleen's cell phone! How did that get there?[60] I didn't have time to think. I just answered it.

---

[60] How do you think? Remember Bitsie's little tussle with Kathleen in the studio? She won – but he knew how to hurt her. He stole her cell phone. Stuck it up his insides and made off with it.

What kind of idiot am I? I *answered* it!

Why didn't I just turn it off? I don't know. I was on automatic, I guess. Like at home when I answer the phone and say, "Sorry, you've got the wrong number. May I take a message?" Who'd leave a message for the wrong number? I say it without thinking.

Same thing here. I just said, "Hello" and tried to ignore the big heavy footsteps pounding down the hall toward me.

"Telly?!?" It was Nick.

"Ah…yeah. It's me."

I could hear Arnold fumbling with the key.

Nick just kept on talking as if the world were a completely normal place to live. "I was in the studio and thought if I phoned Kathleen's cell I could hear the ring and maybe find it for her—but I guess I'm too late."

"Un-huh," I went, not wanting to come right out and lie about anything until I absolutely had to.

I could barely hear Nick over the noise. I didn't know exactly what was happening in the hall, but I guessed that Bitsie must have seen Arnold with the key and attacked him from behind. Now they were banging and smashing and pounding into the door. Plaster was falling down on my head and that little window was rattling like one of those bean-shakers five-year-olds get to play in music class. I almost felt sorry for Arnold. He must have been terrified. Wouldn't you be if a furious, beakless Bitsie attacked you?

"What's all that noise?" Nick asked.

I said, "It's—uh—Kathleen. She's doing her exercises." Not a bad excuse, considering I just came up with it off the top of my head like that.

Nick seemed to find nothing odd about Kathleen doing that much screaming, grunting and slamming into walls as part of her exercise routine.[61] He said, "It'll probably do her good. Better not disturb her."

Arnold and Bitsie must have knocked one of the pictures off the wall because there was a major crash right then.

I guess that's why Nick said, "Unless you think she's going to hurt herself."

I said no, no, she'll be fine, but I didn't really believe it of course. I didn't think Kathleen would ever recover from Friday afternoon—especially once she got a load of the new Bitsie.

"Oh, listen, while I have you on the phone, two things …" I couldn't believe this guy. I spent a month dying to talk to him, but now was the time he chose to chat? "Do you know if Zola managed to get hold of Laird to fix Bitsie up? I'd really like that puppet to be in tip-top shape for Monday's shoot."

I concentrated on lying so I wouldn't throw up. I said, "Oh, that's all taken care of."

"Great." I wished he didn't fall for stuff so easily. "The other thing," he said, "is I just checked our e-mails and you have a whole pile of urgent messages from Bess."

I started to feel like I'd rather just stay there and take my chances with Arnold. I said, "They're not important. Everything is urgent for her."

"Oh, good," he went. "I was worried there for a sec. They all had subject lines like 'Don't do anything stupid!'

---

[61] Come to think of it, most people who knew Kathleen probably wouldn't either.

and 'Stay where you are!' and 'I'm coming to get you!' If I hadn't already heard a few stories about Bess, I probably would have called the cops! Ha-ha!"

Ha-ha. Who was laughing?

"I've got to go," I said. "There's someone at the door."

I wasn't lying.

Bitsie had just walked in.

48

RUNNING ON EMPTY.

We were going to miss the bus! And it was all my fault!

Bitsie just wanted to leave Arnold tied up in that puppet-clothing-rope. It would serve him right, Bitsie said. But I couldn't do that. Who knew if anyone but us ever visited the Great van Gurp? If someone a hundred years from now found a skeleton tied to a chair with tiny pink jackets, how would I feel?

Rotten. [62]

And anyway, Zola had said Arnold was an honest man. She believed there was good in this guy. I wanted to give him the benefit of the doubt. I figured he wasn't the first person the TV business had driven nuts.[63] Someone probably knew how to help him.

When he came to, I told him that.

Sort of.

---

[62] I'd probably feel rotten if I lived to 112 anyway. But that's not my point.
[63] I mean, I already knew at least one other...

By that time I'd taken the rope off and dragged him into his big lopsided bed.[64] I made Bitsie stay out in the hall and keep his mouth shut and I told Arnold that he'd had a seizure. An anti-flatulent diabetic postpartum seizure, I called it, which doesn't actually exist but sounds serious. I told him he'd been hallucinating and saying crazy things about talking puppets and cha-cha lessons and holding people hostage. I patted his hand just like my dad always does (especially with his "difficult" patients) and I told him I was going to get him a doctor.

Then I stuffed Bitsie into my knapsack again and ran like my undies were on fire.

I was at the phone booth by the Petrocan calling 9-1-1[65] when I saw the bus to Toronto fly by.

I gave the lady Arnold's address, hung up and ran.

And I mean ran.

Like I've never run before. I knew it was hopeless, but I kept on running anyway. If I stopped running and just admitted I missed the bus, I was going to have to come up with another plan. That was too terrible to even think about.

So I kept running—even though the bus was half a click ahead of me.

I'd spent a month thinking that the big city and everything about it was so much better than hick towns like the one I'd grown up in. But right then I knew it wasn't true. There are a lot of wonderful things about the country. If you

184

---

[64] For which he owes me, big time. What did that guy eat?

[65] I have to admit, Bitsie was right about that. He'd seen enough police shows to know if I used Kathleen's cell phone they would have been able to trace the call. I didn't need that.

asked me today, I'd list the cows and the beaches and the Turkey Burger off exit 13. But that's not what I was thinking about then.

What I really loved about the backwoods at that moment in time were the country drivers. The type of driver that never breaks 50 k an hour even if his wife is giving birth to triplets in the backseat.

The type that will block traffic for five minutes while he decides whether to turn left and visit Uncle Basil or keep on going straight to the Bingo Hall.

The type that will slow down to zero to admire some roadkill, totally unaware that the Saturday Greyhound to New Cumberland, Goldrink, Neewack and Toronto has had to grind to a halt behind him and, since it was just sitting there doing nothing, let on a tall, skinny girl with stupid orange braids and a wiggling knapsack.

49
EVERYONE HAS A BREAKING POINT.

It was the Choc-o-rama that did it. I was fine until then. Despite everything I'd been through, I didn't cry once.

Not when Kathleen said she got saddled with me. Not when Nick agreed. Not when Bitsie blackmailed me. Not when the police were after us. Not when the guy wouldn't sell me a bus ticket. Not when Arnold kidnapped us. Not when Bitsie tore his nose off.

So no matter what you might think about me, you can't say I'm a sookie-baby. I did pretty well.

Until we got on that stupid bus.

It was completely empty and I could tell the bus driver was sort of hoping to have someone to talk to for a while, but I went right to the very back and flaked out on the seats. I was hoping the Bess movie would just start up again and I could forget everything for a while, but it didn't happen. It was like there was one of those rude, noisy people in the theater, ruining the movie for everybody else. Every time I'd picture some funny little thing Bess did, the guy in my head would scream, "People like that should be locked up!" or "Selfish brat!" or "Another one of her lies!"

I gave up. I considered lying under the seats and pretending it was Dreemland, but the floor was really sticky and I wasn't prepared to spend the rest of my life glued to a Greyhound bus.

I tried to think of something else, but the only thing I could come up with was how hungry I was.

I hadn't eaten in a whole day. More than a whole day. I was starving.

I dumped everything out of my knapsack, hoping I'd maybe find a furry grey mint or a rubbery Cheezie or even a hard little hunk of Mum's tofu brownies left over from school. All I found was a grumpy puppet, a stolen cell phone and a busted-up Choc-o-rama.

I turned off the cell phone and threw it back in my knapsack. I gave Bitsie a look that said "shut up" and he did. I couldn't believe it. He's usually not that sensitive to other people's moods.

Then I picked up the Choc-o-rama.

It had been bent before, but now it was completely broken in two. The wrapper was all torn and dirty. A lot of the "chocolatey coating" had chipped off the "crispy wafer filling" and what was left had gone kind of white, like it had been through a terrible shock or something. It didn't look like a commemorative chocolate bar that anyone would want to keep for the rest of their life even if they'd pledged that they always would, so I decided to eat it.

That's when I started to cry.

It's stupid, I know, but right until that very moment I always sort of believed there was a chance that somehow everything would turn out okay. Even better than okay.

188

Kathleen would be my friend again. Zola wouldn't lose her job. Bitsie would grow a new beak and quit acting so immature. And Nick would…

I don't know exactly what I hoped Nick would do. Not be my boyfriend or ask me out on a date or even take me out for ice cream. I'm not that dumb. He's a grown-up and I'm a kid from Beach Meadows. I guess I just wanted him to notice once more that my eyes matched my T-shirt. That would have been great.

But there I was sitting with a stolen, broken puppet, eating the Choc-o-rama Nick gave me the day I thought everything in my life was just going to keep getting better and better. It didn't taste very good. It didn't fill me up. And pretty soon, no doubt, I'd be pooping it out into a toilet somewhere.

189

No wonder I started to cry.

At first it was just tears dribbling down my face and onto my chocolate bar, but pretty soon I was really sobbing. Sobbing—then making this walrus mating call when I tried to get some air—then sobbing again. It just kept coming and coming and coming.

The bus driver ignored me[66] and Bitsie tried to ignore me for a while too.[67]

But then he did something that really surprised me. He sat on my lap and put his arms around my neck.

He hugged me!

---

[66] I bet he was glad I didn't sit down and talk to him after all.
[67] There's nothing he hates more than bodily fluids, and by that time I was covered in them.

I threw him off. Sure, I'd done a lot of things I wasn't supposed to do, and I'm not saying I wasn't to blame. But I never would have done them if it hadn't been for Bitsie.

If he thought he could just hug me and everything would be absolutely a-okay again, he was crazy. This wasn't TV.

He picked himself up off the floor, climbed onto my lap and hugged me again.

I tried to throw him off again but he managed to hang on with one arm. I pried that arm off, but by the time I did he'd grabbed on with the other one. We did that switch-o-change-o thing for a while and then I just gave up. I let him stay there. If he wanted to get soaked with tears and drool and snot while I sobbed away, fine. Just as long as he didn't ask me to stop.

The only problem was that his antennae and yellow fuzz-ball hair kept getting in my face. I bent down his antennae and that kept them out of my way, but each time I'd push his hair down it would pop back up and get in my nose again. So I had to keep pushing it down.

That's all I was doing.

I know he thought I was patting him—like this was a sign of affection or something—because he hugged me even tighter when I did it, but he was wrong. This wasn't about forgiveness or friendship or anything like that. It was just about that stupid hair of his getting up my nose. If I'd had a pair of scissors, I would have cut it off.

Maybe it fooled me a bit too, though, because the longer we sat there hugging and patting, the more Bitsie seemed like the best friend I ever had. I know you're probably thinking that doesn't say much about my other friends. Who could be worse than a lying, cheating, stealing, arrogant little puppet?

But you know what hit me?

It wasn't his fault. Bitsie honestly didn't know any better. He'd never had a friend. No one had ever cared about him before. How was he supposed to know how friendship worked? He was just figuring things out as he went along. Like the rest of us, I guess.

And so he made some mistakes[68]—so what? I guess we all do when we're learning something. Just think of the clothes I thought were nice before I saw what everyone was wearing in Toronto! It wouldn't be fair to hold them against me now. I didn't realize overalls were so lame. I've learned since then.

I finally stopped sobbing when a man got on at New Cumberland. He looked at me like "Oh-no-I'm-stuck-here-for-four-hours-with-a-nutcase." But that wasn't why I shut up.

I shut up because he sat down and put a newspaper over his face so he could get some sleep, and I saw that front-page picture of Bitsie and me.

[68] Some?!? Like a million. But my point is still the same.

50
WHAT GOOD WOULD THAT DO?

It was the shock of seeing the headline that did it. "Puppet Prodigy Disappears."

I stopped crying. I stopped patting. I just stared at the paper.

It was over. The cops were probably looking for me. They probably thought I stole Bitsie, and no matter what I said they'd never believe the real story. The word "hopeless" popped into my head again. Several times.

I made myself move. I took out Kathleen's cell phone. I was going to call the police. Tell them to pick me up at the next stop. I knew I'd be in big trouble, but at least I'd get something to eat.

The only problem was that the cops would call my parents and then they'd be really worried and probably get upset with Kathleen for not taking better care of me, and then Kathleen would probably fire Zola for not putting Bitsie away herself—and in the end, Bitsie would still have to work at a job he hated.

I realized that turning myself in might be the right thing to do, but no one would be happy if I did it. No one.

Not a soul.

I looked out the window. It was dark. I couldn't see very much. I just kept thinking, No one would be happy if I did.

I decided not to call the police. I decided to fix this mess. I didn't know how, but I was going to try. If it didn't work, they could arrest me then.

For a long time there was just a whole bunch of stupid ideas banging around in my brain like bumper cars. A lot of them started with "I wish everything could just be…!" and a lot of others started with "It's not fair!"

I probably did an hour of that before I had a plan. I realized there were three things I had to do. Quit wasting time wishing everything was going to be perfect again. Quit wasting time thinking everything was a complete disaster. And find out what else it said in the newspaper about me.

It took a while to make out the rest of the article because I had to read it upside down, but basically it was all about Bitsie. ("Don't let the frumpy glasses and the little-girl braids fool you. This puppet is the hottest comedy act to hit the streets of Toronto since Jim Carrey was a rubber-faced boy.") There was also some stuff about my wicked stepfather. Police were apparently trying to "trace the story."

The photo was blurry and only showed my back because I was running away, the description of Bitsie was wrong and nobody could remember what I looked like. I was insulted, of course,[69] but relieved.

194

---

[69] Nobody noticed my green eyes? Or my height? Or even my T-shirt? Kathleen spent $48 for that T-shirt. You'd think someone would have noticed it.

So it wasn't a complete disaster. No one would be able to recognize us.[70]

That was fine, but there was still the problem of Bitsie's nose.

It was 11:30 Saturday night. Bitsie had to be back in the studio with a beak by 7 a.m. Monday. That gave me thirty-one and a half hours to fix his face. I thought maybe if I phoned Laird at The Puppet Plantation he'd be able to do something for us.

I explained the situation to Bitsie.

He stopped hugging me and said, "I'm never going back to that studio and you can't make me!"

He was right. I couldn't. Not after all we'd been through.

195

---

[70] I hoped.

51

I JUST WENT FOR IT.

Okay. I could deal with that. It just required a slight change in plans.

I grabbed Bitsie and the cell phone and went into the washroom at the back of the bus. I locked the door and told Bitsie what we were going to do. He had that look on his face—the one Bess uses to say "No matter what you ask me to do, I'm not going to like it." He came around, though, once he realized that I was doing this for him.

I dialed the Puppet Plantation number and handed the phone to Bitsie. We were lucky Laird had no life. It was midnight Saturday but he was at the shop working on some drawings for a new puppet.

Bitsie said, "Hey, Laird," in Zola's voice, "glad I caught you."

I *knew* Laird had a crush on her! You should have heard him. "Well, I'm glad you caught me too, Zola. How can I help you?" He sounded like such a cool guy, you'd almost think he was used to talking to girls.

"I know it's short notice," "Zola" said, "but we need a new Bitsie double."

"No problem," he went. "For when?"

"Monday morning by 6:30?" Bitsie made it sound like Zola was really apologetic for imposing. It was perfect.

Laird hemmed and hawed for a while, saying he could only do it if the molds were in good shape and he had the correct type of latex for the job on hand, etc. etc. etc. I was in agony. I was kicking myself for wasting all that time crying and not thinking of this sooner. Finally, Laird said, "…but, yeah, I think I could get it done if I start right now."

I got "Zola" to ask how much it would be. Laird did the old "Same as usual" but then, no doubt just to keep "Zola" on the phone a bit longer, he figured it out for her.

"It'll be $2036.42. That's including the tax."

Now all I had to do was find the $2036.42.

51

I CAN COME UP WITH DUMB IDEAS AS WELL AS THE REST OF THEM.

It took me all night to figure out where to get the money. That's because I got stuck on the idea of having a bake sale.

How stupid was that? How many Rice Krispie squares was I going to have to sell by Monday morning to raise $2036.42? About a bazillion—and frankly, I didn't have a pan that big.

Then I thought of chocolate bar sales. That was stupid too. Our entire school sold chocolate bars for a month and all we got out of it was $864 and a lot of pimples.

Once I got back to the studio and raided the staff fridge I was able to think a bit more clearly. I guess I just needed to get my mind off food.

Busking was obviously out. So was blackmailing—despite Bitsie's "foolproof" plan to frame Mel. In fact, all of Bitsie's plans were out. They all involved something illegal—arson, smuggling, insurance fraud, grand theft auto, you name it.

When I said no to another one of his ideas,[70] Bitsie stomped off in a big huff to watch TV. Like this wasn't his problem too.

---

[70] He actually suggested we try forging the Mona Lisa and selling it. The guy watches too much TV.

I needed to come up with some fast, easy way to make money. A paper route? Baby-sitting? Lawn-mowing? As far as I could see, nothing a twelve-year old could do brought in that type of money. It didn't seem fair. It was so easy for grown-ups. I thought about that woman who came up with the idea for a television series about doorknobs. It couldn't have taken her more than about six minutes to dream up something that lame, and Kathleen was about to give her $5000 for it!

Boy, that annoyed me—until I realized the possibilities.

52
SEE?

My Home Is My Hovel—A series that visits the homes of unbelievably messy people.

Wipe Your Feet First!—A series that visits the homes of unbelievably neat people.

House of Horrors—Got a neighbor you hate? Well, it's payback time. We'll surprise them with a free renovation. You pick the colors…

Live Like a King—Every week we explore the home of a different family named King. Do they really live differently from the rest of us?

Homes of the Criminally Insane—If you lived here, you'd go nuts too.

Was That You?—A twenty-six part series about household odors.

Below-Bed Living—For people who like lying under their beds and pretending the world does not exist.

Dirty Secrets—Why spend all that time cleaning the house when, with a few simple techniques, you can learn to cover the grime?

By Sunday morning, I'd come up with a pile of ideas. A lot of them were pretty stupid. I just didn't know if they were the kind of stupid that got on TV or not. I decided to drag Bitsie away from the Shopping Channel for a few minutes to find out what he thought. He was an expert after all.

"Come up with a decorating show idea for Kathleen?!?" he said in this really snarky voice. "That's how you think you're going to make the money?!?"

I knew Bitsie was just being rude because I didn't like his idea about blackmailing Mel or stealing cars. But he was so sarcastic it really bugged me. He went, "Well, how about this, then? 'Obsessive-Compulsive Home: For the Mentally Unstable Decorator'—Kathleen would lo-ove that one!"

Bitsie started laughing his head off. "Would you quit that?" I said. "You don't have to act like Kathleen's nuts just because she's particular about her living quarters. If you knew anything, you'd know there are lots of people like that!"

I was just making it sound like I knew more than he did because, frankly, I didn't like his attitude. But then I thought, Hey, I bet there are...

53

FOR SALE:
ONE SLIGHTLY USED KIDNEY.

Kathleen sounded a bit iffy at first. You could hardly blame her. Here was Laird MacAdam trying to sell her an interior design show. Believe me, Laird was hardly a guy you'd want to take decorating tips from—unless you really went for that black-walls-and-leftover-pizza look he seemed to like.

But it was the only way my plan would work. If Kathleen bought the series idea, she wouldn't just hand over a whack of cash. She'd write a check. So I had to get her to make it out to Laird so we could pay him for the new puppet double.

That meant Bitsie had to pretend he was Laird.

With a decorating idea.

Sure, it was a bit of a stretch, but we had no other choice—unless I wanted to sell a kidney, of course.[72]

I knew right away Kathleen was interested. "Obsessive-Compulsive Home" was perfect for her and all those other people out there whose coat hangers have to match their bedspreads. But she was hesitating. I thought maybe she

---

[72] My parents were always pretty reasonable with me, but I figured they'd draw the line at me selling my organs.

didn't have the money, so I got Bitsie to say that normally he'd charge $5000 for a series idea, but for this weekend only he was offering it at the bargain-basement price of just $2036.42!

I really thought she was going to go for it this time, but then she said, "Laird, I'm sorry. I'm really interested in your idea but I don't know if I can make a decision right now. I'm too distracted. I haven't seen Telly all weekend."

She noticed. I was so happy.

On second thought, she noticed! I was in trouble!

Kathleen was really blabbing away now. "I had a very, ahhhhh, 'stressful' day Friday[73] so I slept a lot this weekend. I thought maybe Telly just went to bed after me and got up before me. She's very independent, you know. Very responsible. But now I'm starting to worry. Her bed doesn't look slept in. I wonder if I should call the police."

The police!!!!

I shook my head wildly, and Bitsie said, "No, no. I wouldn't do that because…" then there was this really long pause while I scribbled down what to say next, "because I just saw Telly half an hour ago! She was staying with Zola this weekend and they came in to get some work done on Bitsie. In fact, she was the one who told me you were looking for ideas for a new series."

Kathleen was so relieved she bought the idea on the spot.

I turned off the cell phone and smiled at Bitsie. How long since I'd done that?

---

[73] No kidding.

54

JUST LIKE ON THE HEALTH CHANNEL.

There was just one more thing to do. Operate on Bitsie.

I thought it was going to be easy. I just had to take out his mecs and put them in the old puppet double. Bitsie'd seen it done a million times so he was going to walk me through it. He would have done it himself, of course, but those four-fingered foam hands of his weren't really suited to surgery.

The problem was I'd stepped on his head. Remember? I wasn't thinking about his mecs then. I was just thinking about getting him out that window. So all those little rods and springs that a normal puppet needs to move his eyes and flutter his eyelids were completely banged up. Ruined. Useless.

I admit it. I had a little cry about that. I was so tired by then. I just couldn't face one more thing.

Bitsie didn't hug me this time, but he did scamper off to the staff lounge and bring me some food. Somebody's lunch from 1995 by the looks of it, but I ate it anyway. You know that story about the Canadian doctor who let something go bad by mistake and then realized he'd discovered this amazing new medicine. It was like that. Maybe there's something in really, really old spaghetti that gives you superhuman energy. Or maybe I just needed a break. Or maybe it just seemed really stupid to give up now.

I don't know. But I scraped the fuzzy green stuff off and ate the spaghetti and suddenly I felt like I could do anything.

I got out Zola's toolbox. I saved what I could of Bitsie's mecs and found some rods and springs and screws in an old workshop. Anything I was still missing I scavenged from Ram. I knew he wasn't in Monday's show so I could fix him later. Bitsie and I crawled under the beach house set, where we wouldn't have to worry about the security guard finding us, and got to work.

By about two in the morning, we had the mecs in and the old double working about as well as Bitsie on a bad day. One eye didn't always close and the other one tended to wander off to the right, but he could have passed.

I could have got some sleep then, but I didn't. After everything Bitsie and I had put Zola and Kathleen through, we owed them a working puppet.

By quarter after six, that old double could do the Macarena better than Bitsie. Bitsie wasn't one hundred percent pleased with that, but I was proud of myself.

I went to the washroom to tidy up. That's when I realized that I still had those stupid braids on my head. I took them off and looked in the mirror. It was funny. My face hadn't changed, but I barely recognized myself. I had to say, "So this is me" a couple of times before it felt right.

But then it did feel right. It was a nice feeling, knowing who you are—for a while at least.

55

MORE OR LESS
THE WAY IT WENT.

I don't know if I'll ever figure out exactly what happened next. Everything went so fast and it was all such a shock, but I'll do my best to explain.

Laird arrived just like he said he would at 6:30 in the morning with the new Bitsie double, and I thought I was home free.

That was until Laird said he wanted to give it to Zola personally.

I couldn't believe it. Laird's stupid hopeless crush was going to ruin my life! My stomach went mushy. What was I going to do?

Laird had even shaved,[74] so I knew he had no intention of leaving. In situations like that, you can't wait until a brilliant idea comes to you. You just have to do the best you can in the time you've got.

That's my excuse.

I told Laird that Zola had come down with a really bad case of diarrhea[75] and wouldn't be in that day. I was just

---

[74] Though not very well. He obviously hadn't had much practice.
[75] It was the first thing I thought of. I guess because of that mushy stomach of mine.

promising him that a check would be in the mail by the end of the week and pushing him out the door when who walks in but Zola.

Laird sucked his belly in and said, "Why, hello, feeling better are you?"

I thought it was all over then, but Zola said, "Sorry, Laird, I can't talk now. I've got to run!"

Laird, of course, understood, given her little "problem" and all, and I thought I was home free again, until I realized Zola had to run because Kathleen was at the end of the hall, waving at her to come.

I grabbed the puppet double, slammed the door behind Laird and raced after Zola. Kathleen was just saying, "Zola, I wanted to thank you for taking Telly."

I thought it was all over again, but then Kathleen saw me and stopped and ran over and gave me a big hug. "I missed you," she said, and this time I knew she meant it. "I have this really neat series idea I wanted to talk to you about!"

I smiled. I couldn't honestly say I missed her—I'd been a little busy for that—but I was really glad to see her again.

"So, tell me," she went on, "did the two of you have fun this weekend?"

And I thought it was all over again.

But before Zola could say, "I was away with my boyfriend," Nick came flying in.

"Kathleen! I really need to talk to you!" he said. "Why weren't you answering your cell phone?"

Kathleen went, "Cell phone?!?" like "What's the matter with you? You were with me when I lost it." Then Nick looked at me like "Didn't you give it back to her?" and I thought it was all over again, but he said, "It doesn't matter! Dorothy and Mitch caught the early plane to try and find Bess. They're going to be here any minute."

My parents were coming!?! Bess was missing! Kathleen looked as shocked as I did.

Then Nick said, "And there's a commotion at the front desk you have to deal with."

But the commotion wasn't at the front desk anymore. A second later it was in the hall with us and its name was Bess and it was screaming and elbowing a security guard in the head and running right for me.

"Telly! Telly! You're okay! You're okay!"

Bess practically knocked me over. She was hugging and kissing me, and that poor security guard was sort of caught in the middle, not sure if he should arrest Bess or hug her back. She was crying and babbling something about the e-mail I sent her and knowing right away I was going to do something I shouldn't and that it was all her fault because she'd been such a bad role model and seeing my picture in the paper and stealing her ex-boyfriend's father's Winnebago and driving nonstop to find me because she'd kill herself if anything ever happened to me.

And Kathleen and Zola and Nick were just cluing into what was going on and trying to find out more about that picture in the paper when my parents came barging in and saw Bess and me locked in this big wet hug.

I realize now that they must have been sick with worry over both of us, especially after reading those e-mails. But when I looked up and saw my parents there, they were both smiling. Smiling at the sight of us hugging and crying. They were crying too, of course, but mostly they were smiling and looking at us like we'd just won first place for piano duet in the Kiwanis Music Festival or something.

Like we were the two best daughters anyone could ever ask for.

I'm just glad Bitsie was hidden safely away in my knapsack because, believe me, the whole sappy scene would have been enough to make him throw up.

EPILOGUE:
THEN WHAT HAPPENED?

It's two years later now. I'm back in Beach Meadows. I'm in Grade Nine. I'm still shy, but I did talk to a boy yesterday. ("You dropped your pencil." It's not much, I know, but it's a start.) My language arts teacher is really impressed with how "imaginative" my writing has become.

Bitsie'n'Bytesie got renewed for one more season. Production didn't go into overtime once.

Kathleen has a huge hit on her hands with *Obsessive-Compulsive Home*. Laird has no idea why she keeps thanking him when she wins yet another award for Excellence in Lifestyle Broadcasting. When Kathleen's lonely, she calls me. We usually just talk about new trends in window treatments and closet organizers, but it's always nice to hear her voice.

Zola lied and told Kathleen I spent that weekend with her. I never had to ask her to do it and she never asked me to explain. Zola said she knows I only did what I felt I had to do. No wonder I love her.

Nick married his girlfriend and it didn't bother me a bit. I did crawl into Dreemland when I found out, but I was planning on doing that anyway.

Arnold van Gurp is pitching a television series about a puppet who comes to life as a dance instructor. He has several broadcasters interested in it.

Mum doesn't talk about the time Bess stole the Winnebago and drove nonstop to Toronto. She talks about Bess's "rescue mission." She's very proud of her, even though she can't understand for the life of her why Bess would have thought that blurry picture in the paper was of me.

Dad got a tattoo and now Bess and he have a lot more to talk about.

Bess is doing community service at the children's hospital instead of jail time. She's really good with the patients. They love her "energy." Sometimes I come along with her and bring my puppet. His name is Gord. He has black hair and a black mustache and a completely normal nose.

Only a few kids with really high fevers have ever suspected that he might just be Bitsie.

ABOUT THE AUTHOR

Photo credit: John Sherlock

The Puppet Wrangler is funny and fast-paced and set against the fascinating backdrop of the television industry, a world that the author, Gemini-winning **Vicki Grant,** knows well. She is the writer and creative director of *Scoop & Doozie*, a TV puppet show. Jim Rankin was one of the puppeteers on the show. "Between takes," Vicki says, "Jim's puppet 'Doozie' would carry on conversations with the crew, conversations that showed a whole different side of the little orange bulldozer. Very funny, but definitely not preschool material. Bitsie owes a huge debt of gratitude to Jim Rankin." *The Puppet Wrangler* is Vicki's first novel.

Vicki's got a cool website, check it out at www.vickigrant.com

Watch for this new Orca novel coming soon to a bookstore or library near you!

Barkerville Gold
Dayle Campbell Gaetz

Fresh from capturing daring art thieves in *Mystery from History*, Rusty, Katie and Sheila are back. This time the trio is in historic Barkerville, a gold rush town with a secret. After witnessing what they take to be a ghost in the night, the three friends find themselves involved in a mystery from the past that has a few others interested as well. New information has come to light about a fortune in missing gold, a centuries-old curse and a missing miner. The three budding detectives are in a race against time to recover the gold and return it to its rightful owners to avert a tragedy.

Don't miss these other exciting juvenile fiction titles from Orca Book Publishers

Cougar Cove
by Julie Lawson

Barkerville Gold
by Dayle Campbell Gaetz

Mystery from History
by Dayle Campbell Gaetz

The Scream of the Hawk
by Nancy Belgue

The Gramma War
by Kristin Butcher

In the Clear
by Anne Laurel Carter

Leaving the Log House
by Ainslie Manson

My Name Is Mitch
by Shelagh Lynne Supeene

**Book One in
The Summer of Magic Quartet:**
The White Horse Talisman
by Andrea Spalding

**Book Two in
The Summer of Magic Quartet:**
Dance of the Stones
by Andrea Spalding